IELTS

雅思寫作聖經

模擬試題

韋爾 ◎ 著

《劍17》核心話題和 暢銷書論點 加持
穩拿 9.0高分

依樣葫蘆，靈活組織出佳作

藉由書中**延伸規劃範文**，立即掌握**《劍16》**和**《劍17》核心話題**，飛快組織出論點並導向其中一個結論，完成考試要求。

段落拓展和切入主題規劃，迅速抓住考官眼球

納入**20篇大作文範文**，巧妙運用各類型切入句，舖陳並豐富化首段論述，一次就獲取**9.0寫作佳績**。

Editor's preface

作者序

隨著《劍16》和《劍17》的推出，相信考生都能感受到一點，也就是在大作文的寫作主題上都較難發揮，而小作文則近似於前面出現過的雙表格題或是考生熟悉的主題，所以在這本書的規劃上會以《劍16》和《劍17》話題為核心，規劃實戰主題和模擬試題兩個部分。實戰主題是跟《劍16》和《劍17》大作文主題近似的考題，但有助於考生延續這些主題，在寫作和口說分數上都能有顯著的進步。

現在就以其中一篇延續規劃的主題來解釋應用的部分。《劍17 TEST1 W2》的題目Do you think the advantages of taking risks outweigh the disadvantages?，考生可以運用書中規劃的近似主題延續答關於**taking risks**的相關主題。且書中規劃的主題幾乎每篇均有「**搭配暢銷書觀點**」，除了更具說服力外，在切入主題和延伸應用在近似或其他相關話題都能出奇制勝。**❶首段先由暢銷書觀點切入主題，而非改寫或重述題目**（大多數考生在第一段都是採取改寫題目來進行切入一個主題，也就是運用paraphrase，但更佳的範文不會運用這個方法）。由暢銷書觀點可以得到「投報率的多寡」，進而引出與另一本暢銷書觀點吻合的陳述。最後，才拉回正題，也就是要如何權衡風險。**❷次段使用暢銷書實例**，「冒風險的同時亦傾向於能獲取更佳的成功結果是較好的選擇。」得到權衡風險的折衷辦法。在進一步說明要如何「魚和熊掌兼得」。分別在兩所學校得到所具備的知識。❸**在風險權衡中，捨棄名校思維**，因為在不提供獎學金的前提下，會讓自己畢業後就有負債的風險。❹**運用hedging這個概念**，但也指出了「降低風險增加了你能夠獲取想要的結果的成功機率，但是你必須要放棄掉能得到更好結果的可能。」

（在❶-❹，你會發現是有一個寫作切入、鋪陳和邏輯順序在，而非反覆描述許多類似的文意或是很模糊的語句。另外一點是，在當中的描述和舉例中，你能迅速應用在其他話題。例如「捨棄名校思維」、「不提供獎學金」，你能用於自己的自傳或是口語話題，表達出你只在提供獎學金的前提下，才考慮該學校，或是在外商求職面試中，表達你希望是工作一陣子後，公司能支付你前往知名理工大學繼續進修。單一在這個範文裡就有非常多可以加以運用的點。最後是，你會發現這個延伸話題的範文是在講述**權衡風險**的觀點和看法，而《劍17 TEST1 W2》的題目是要你寫出**「利大於弊」**、**「弊大於利」**，所以你可以運用範文中的論述，迅速組織出你對承擔風險的看法，最後漸漸導向你想要的結論，也就是「利大於弊」或「弊大於利」的結尾，然後符合考試的task accomplishment）。

除了前面提到過的切入主題的部分，書中也特別強化「如何切入主題」，某些原因是許多考生並未於寫作課中學習到要如何切入一個主題。而另一個主因是，教授們看報告或考官看範文其實只要看考上第一段寫的前幾句就知道這篇會是大概落於哪個分數段的文章，甚至不用費心看完。（就像每本劍橋雅思題本後方提供的像是

5.5分的小作文範文。考官看久了，那樣類似的文句就是5-5.5分的文章。）以某篇延伸範文為例，當中提供了❶**先鋪陳並豐富化切入句**，「新品牌的手搖飲料店如雨後春筍般不斷地浮現在已經飽和的市場裡，但是手搖飲料店家們在某些程度上懂得要如何操控消費者。」❷**加入譬喻和嘲諷**，在Instagram上上傳過時飲品的照片的話，人們會想到你到底是住在哪個星球上。❸**推論出，飲料公司就是意識到這點，所以操控奏效**。（與先前的，以暢銷書文句作為切入句不同，反而以近似觀察者或報章雜誌口吻切入這個主題。這篇範文也能應用在《劍16 TEST3 W2》的題目Sugary products should be made more expensive to encourage people to consume less sugar. Do you agree?，考生可以運用範文的論點融合並組織自己的看法快速寫成約200字主要的兩個段落，最後只要加上是否同意的該論點，寫最後70-100字完成最後一段。表明同意或不同意都不影響評分，主要是檢測考生的英語水平和論點的表達。書中共有**20個**大作文範文，可以提供考生模擬和應用在劍橋雅思試題和實際考試中，相信對於備考成效顯著。

另外要說明的是，背誦範文對英語水平會有顯著提升，不過直接背誦整篇並在考場中照寫，還是有可能被考官判定成抄襲。或許適時用部分佳句和加入自己的看法，並再請英文較好的友人或師長潤飾過會更好，整體文章也會更為自然。如果本身寫作程度已經能考到6.5-7.0的考生，相信在看過書籍後，能迅速掌握所有考點，直接應考。）

而若是你在面對科技類話題非常畏懼，在書中《劍17 TEST4 W2》的題目driverless cars也能迅速提升你的實戰力。（因為很可能你在這次的雅思考試大作文中遇到這樣的話題而寫作分數沒有考好。在下一次考試，卻是在口說的第三部分遇到這樣的話題，你又因為口說單項分數被拉低，而至少還要再報考第三次，而且第三次還要很順利。）最後祝所有考生都能獲取佳績。

韋爾 敬上

Instructions 使|用|說|明

UNIT 04 三圓餅圖題：三項飲品在各時段的飲用比例

Writing Task 1

You should spend about 20 minutes on this task

The diagram below includes three pie charts. Each pie chart represents a major drink in Taiwan. The percentage of the consumption of three drinks in four major meals can actually reveal people's habits and preference for drinks in a specific timeframe.

Summarize the information by selecting and reporting the main features, and make comparisons where relevant.

Write at least 150 words

整合能力強化 ❶ 實際演練

請搭配左頁的題目和下方的圖片進行圖表題寫作的演練。

Percentage of the pearl milk tea, coffee, and green tea in typical meals consumed in Taiwan

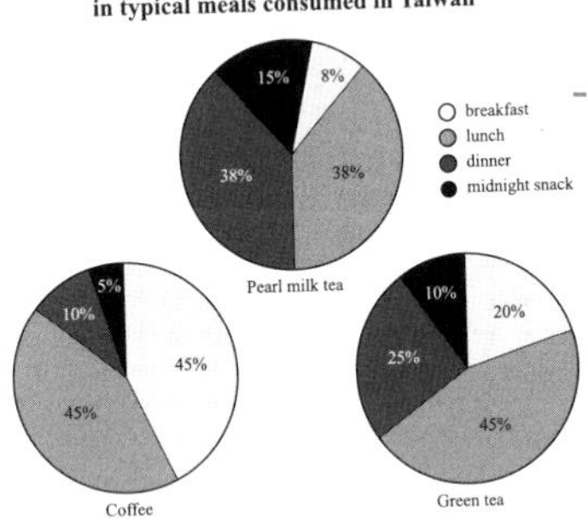

《劍 16》和《劍 17》話題加持
圖表題亦包含循環出題考點
口說和寫作兩個單項分數同步飆升

- 圖表題涵蓋各類別常見的循環出題考點，且每個範文都包含段落拓展，有效協助自學考生組織段落，並適時運用句型搭配陳述出高分句子。

有效點出眾多考生寫作分數卡在 6.5 分的原因
大幅強化應答實力

- ❶熟悉「圖表題常考字彙」跟其反義詞的用法、❷能靈活使用「圖表題常考字彙」其他詞性的用法並強化時態表達❸與「高階形容詞」做搭配❹把敘述具體化❺學習高階圖表題動詞的使用❻搭配同位語表達❼搭配其他句型和❽比較差異處等等。

Instructions 使｜用｜說｜明

 整合能力強化 ❸ 段落拓展

TOPIC

We have been misled into believing that those elite athletes do not necessarily have to work industriously. They are naturally born that way, but that is so not true. They all have received excellent trainings. In addition to their innate talents, what are other factors that you deem might help them outshine other athletes. Use specific reasons and examples to back up your standpoints.

搭配的暢銷書

- The Power of Habit: why we do what we do and how to change《為什麼我們這樣生活，那樣工作？》

Step 1
- 先定義「運動員都具有完美的肌肉組織，而且毫秒之差就會決定最終的贏家。」
- 然後反思，如果是這樣子的話，要贏得比賽，哪個因素實際上會扮演更重要的角色呢？

108

Step 2
- 接著鋪陳，「不論是在電視上或是在巨型的體育館中，我們大多數的人都曾看過一些菁英運動員。獨特的燈光打在他們完美的體態上讓我們都忘卻了他們訓練所付出的苦工。
- 最後導入主題，不過在日常生活中，我們鮮少將像是慣例、習慣和管理風險列入加以思考，而這也是鑑別優劣的原因。

Step 3
- 敘述，並排除掉天賦影響運動員表現。

Step 4
- 搭配暢銷書舉例，並指出「要充分準備且能面對未知是關鍵所在」。
- 得出另一個結論，深夜的密西根湖中游泳訓練和維持表現穩定性，「進一步得出替任何意料之外的事情作足準備比起訓練時的強度和運動員體內的肌肉數量多寡等等的都更為重要。」
- 最後強化論點，習慣和慣例的運動排程對於一個運動員能夠處於狀態良好的情況和準備就緒參賽扮演了重要的角色。

Step 5
- 最後簡短地總結。

Part 2 雅思寫作Task2：《劍16》真題重現《劍17》和

109

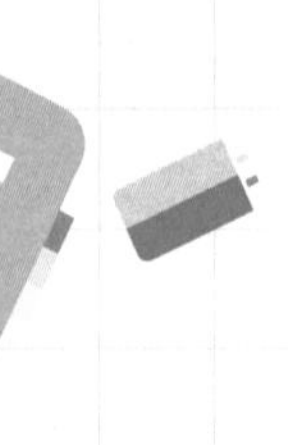

收錄20個大作文主題，涵蓋各類別的段落拓展表達
強化考生組織和邏輯表達英文的能力，自學就能搞定雅思寫作

- 以Unit 3 話題為例，就包含了定義、反思、鋪陳、導入主題、敘述、搭配暢銷書舉例、得出另一個結論和最後強化論點。

❶先定義「運動員都具有完美的肌肉組織，而且毫秒之差就會決定最終的贏家。」

❷然後反思，如果是這樣子的話，要贏得比賽，哪個因素實際上會扮演更重要的角色呢？

❸接著鋪陳，「不論是在電視上或是在巨型的體育館中，我們大多數的人都曾看過一些菁英運動員。獨特的燈光打在他們完美的體態上讓我們都忘卻了他們訓練所付出的苦工。

❹最後導入主題，不過在日常生活中，我們鮮少將像是慣例、習慣和管理風險列入加以思考，而這也是鑑別優劣的原因。

❺敘述，並排除掉天賦影響運動員表現。

❻搭配暢銷書舉例，並指出「要充分準備且能面對未知是關鍵所在」。

❼得出另一個結論，深夜的密西根湖中游泳訓練和維持表現穩定性，「進一步得出替任何意料之外的事情作足準備比起訓練時的強度和運動員體內的肌肉數量多寡等等的都更為重要。」

❽最後強化論點，習慣和慣例的運動排程對於一個運動員能夠處於狀態良好的情況和準備就緒參賽扮演了重要的角色。

Instructions 使|用|說|明

整合能力強化 ❹ 參考範文 ▶MP3 021

經由先前的演練後，現在請看整篇範文並聆聽音檔

In *Mistakes I Made at Work*, Kim Gordon mentions "The idea of "work-life balance" is not necessarily helpful. If you are immersed in your work and raising a family, you might feel a lot of good things – but it may not include balanced." The statement seems to inform us that seeking a work-life balance job is so unlikely, and this is so discouraging. Another expert, a senior director at Goldman Sachs said "the more you talk about work-life balance, the more you create the problem that you want to solve." This further validates there is going to be an ensuing problem when you seek this kind of job. But does the job of work-life balance not exist?

在《我工作中所犯的錯誤中》，金・古登提到「工作－生活平衡的想法並不總是有助益」。如果你沉浸在你的工作和養育一個家庭，你可能會感覺到許多好事情 – 但是可能不會包含平衡」。這個陳述似乎是告知我們追求工作和生活平衡的工作是不可能的，而這是令人沮喪的。另一位專家，一位高勝資深經理說道「你越是談論到工作和生活平衡，你越是創造出你想要解決的問題」。這進一步地證實了，會有接踵而來的問題，當你找尋那樣的工作時。但是工作和生活中平衡的工作是否存在？

242

Unit 06 在工作和生活中取得平衡，思考方式重要嗎？

What experts have told us do have some valid and insightful points, but regardless of what experts tell us, the job of work-life balance does exist. It is the dream job, and it is not something that you seek. This puzzles many of us. But it is like what is described in the book, dream job is often created than found. Normally, it is not the job that you see on the job search pages. This could be the job for someone who has irreplaceable technical skills and job experiences, and recruiters deem you can be the one to do the job. But in the company, they do not have that kind of job title yet. The job is designed for someone who might have the skill to do things that can meet the future goals of the company. This kind of the job is exceptionally rare.

專家們已經告訴我們的確實是有些根據和洞察性的重點，但是不論專家們告訴我們什麼，工作和生活中取得平衡的工作確實存在著。這是夢幻工作，而非你追求而來的工作。這使我們大多數的人感到困惑。但這像是書中所述，夢幻工作通常是創造出來的，而非找到的。通常，這不是在你找工作的頁面中會看到的。但在公司中尚未有這個頭銜的工作存在。這可能是個替有些具有不可取代的專業技巧和工作經驗者所打造的，而招募者認為你是唯一一個可以做那個工作的人。這份工作是一些具有能力，可能能夠達到公司未來目標者所設計的。這樣的工作是相當罕見的。

Part 3 雅思寫作 Task2：大作文

243

暢銷書話題加持，內建「西方寫作邏輯腦」，下筆快如神，
無懼難答的口說和寫作話題，寫出與眾不同文章、驚艷考官

- 收錄給力暢銷書佳句，強化論點具體度和説服力，適時運用於寫作中，亦增添寫作風采，讓考官直接給9.0高分。
- 獨家規劃寫作也搭配錄音，**Task 1** 圖表題寫作和**Task 2** 大作文均附錄音，滿足更多「聽力」學習型的學習者，用零碎的時間就能準備好雅思寫作雙題型。
  - ***Mistakes I Made at Work***《我在工作中所犯的錯誤》
  - ***The Defining Decade***《關鍵十年》
  - ***The Job*** 《工作》
  - ***Rich Dad Poor Dad***《富爸爸窮爸爸》
  - ***What I Wish I Knew When I was 20***《但願當我 20 歲時就知道的事》
  - ***How Will You Measure Your Life***《你如何衡量你的人生》
  - ***The Promise of the Pencil : how an ordinary person can create an extraordinary change"***《一支鉛筆的承諾：一位普通人如何能創造出驚人的改變》
  - ***Desperate Housewives***《慾望師奶》
  - ***The Millionaire Fastlane***《百萬富翁快車道》
  - ***The Personal MBA 10th Anniversary Edition***《不花錢讀名校MBA（第10版周年紀念版）》
  - ***An Economist Walks into a Brothel：And Other Unexpected Places to Understand Risk***《為什麼最便宜的機票不要買？：經濟學家教你降低生活中每件事的風險，做出最好的選擇》

Part 1 雅思寫作 Task1：圖表題小作文

CONTENTS

Part 2 雅思寫作實戰 Task 2：《劍 17》和《劍 16》真題重現

Part 3 雅思寫作 Task2：大作文

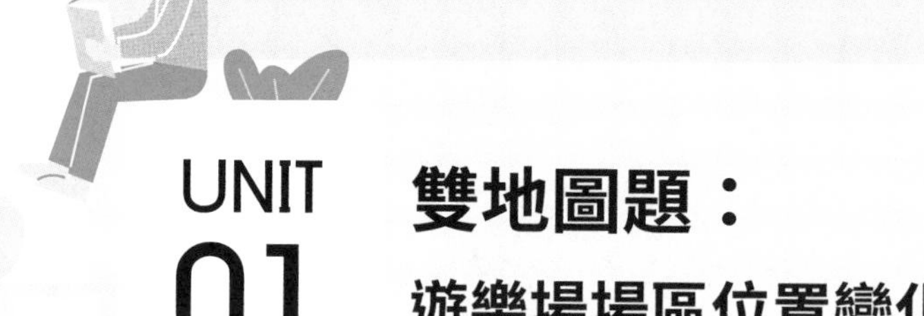

UNIT 01 雙地圖題：遊樂場場區位置變化圖

Writing Task 1

You should spend about 20 minutes on this task

The diagram below shows an amusement park that opened in 2018 and it contained six main facilities. To counter with growing tourists, the owner has discussed with several engineers about the renovation of the amusement park in 2035. Discuss several changes about these two.

Summarize the information by selecting and reporting the main features, and make comparisons where relevant.

Write at least 150 words

整合能力強化 ❶ 實際演練

請搭配左頁的題目和下方的圖片進行圖表題寫作的演練。

Amusement Park 2018

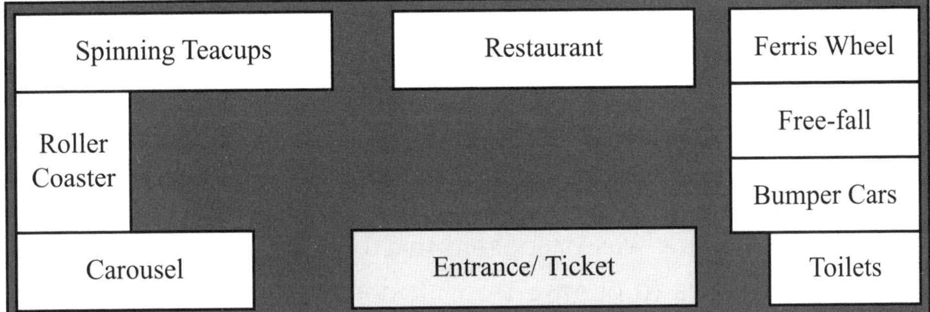

Amusement Park 2035

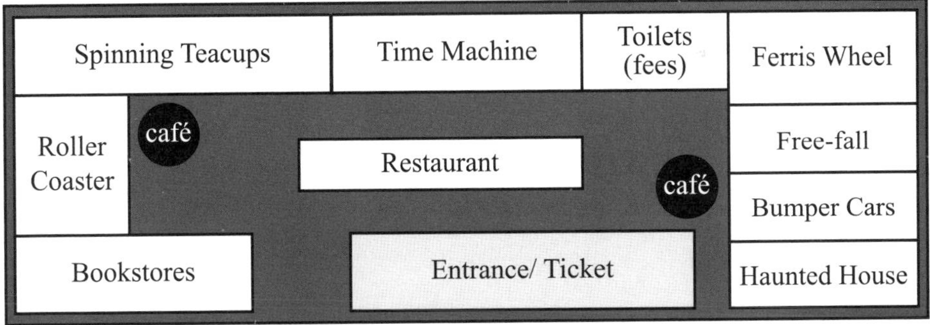

整合能力強化 ❷ 單句中譯英演練

❶ 遊樂園原創於 2018 年，是個長方形區塊包含著六個主要設施提供選擇。它包含了典型的設施，一般的遊樂園都有：旋轉咖啡杯、雲霄飛車、旋轉木馬、摩天輪、自由落體和碰碰車。

____

____

【參考答案】

Amusement Park was originated in 2018, a rectangular area that had six features to choose from. It consisted of typical features that normal amusement parks have: spinning teacups, roller coaster, carousel, Ferris wheel, free-fall, and bumper cars.

❷ 引人注目的是廁所的地點已經從接近入口處移至時光機和摩天輪中間，而且是要收費的，這是史無前例的。

____

____

【參考答案】

It is intriguing to note that the location of the toilets has moved from near the entrance to between Time Machine and Ferris Wheel, and are charged with fees, unprecedentedly.

❸ 從所提供的資訊，位於入口處左側的旋轉木馬在 2035 年時會被書店所取代。

____

____

【參考答案】

From the information provided, carousel situated at the left of the entrance will be replaced by bookstores in 2035.

❹ 另一項會新增的設施是時光機，而愛好者可以體驗回到過去特定時間點的特效。

____

____

【參考答案】

Another feature that will be joined is Time Machine, and fans can experience special effects of going back to a specific timeframe.

❺ 兩個咖啡廳也會新增以迎合日益增加的參觀者，而餐廳將會移至遊樂園的中間處。

____

____

【參考答案】

Two cafes will be added to encounter a growing number of visitors, whereas restaurants will be moving to the middle of the amusement park.

TOPIC

The diagram below shows an amusement park that opened in 2018 and it contained six main facilities. To counter with growing tourists, the owner has discussed with several engineers about the renovation of the amusement park in 2035. Discuss several changes about these two.

Summarize the information by selecting and reporting the main features, and make comparisons where relevant.

Step 1 這題的話要注意有兩個地圖並要注意時間點，因為這影響到時態的使用，重點也是放在比較這兩個圖形的異同。通常時間點是在兩個過去的時間點，這題的第二個地圖是在 2035 年，所以要使用表示未來的時態。有了這些概念並知道要注意時態表達後就可以開始描述了。

Step 2 兩個地圖中沒有變動的部分和新增的設施都是描述點。先描述第一個地圖和主要的遊樂設施。

Step 3 接著描述接下來遊樂園會經歷的改變，有五個主要設施和入口處是維持不變的部分，再來描述新增的部分，廁所的移動和將會收費（這是史無前例的），還有時光機和鬼屋的新增，書店會取代旋轉木馬，和時光機特色的描述，咖啡廳的增加以應對日增的遊客。

Step 4 最後總結出，遊樂園會經歷的改變和簡略描述改變處，最後結尾描述一項特色，例如咖啡廳的增加能夠提升體驗。

整合能力強化 ❹ 參考範文 ▶ *MP3 001*

經由先前的演練後，現在請看整篇範文並聆聽音檔

Amusement Park was originated in 2018, **a rectangular area** that had six features to choose from. It consisted of typical features that normal amusement park have: spinning teacups, roller coaster, carousel, Ferris wheel, free-fall, and bumper cars.

遊樂園原創於 2018 年，是個長方形區塊包含著六個主要設施提供選擇。它包含了典型的設施，一般的遊樂園都有：旋轉咖啡杯、雲霄飛車、旋轉木馬、摩天輪、自由落體和碰碰車。

According to the source, Amusement Park **will be undergoing** a series of changes to meet the demand of those picky fans. In 2035, five main features and the entrance will remain in the same location. It is **intriguing** to note that the location of the toilets has moved from near the entrance to between Time Machine and Ferris Wheel, and unprecedentedly are charged with fees. From the information provided, carousel situated at the left of the entrance **will be replaced by** bookstores in 2035. Another feature that will be joined is Time Machine, and fans can experience special effects of going back to a specific timeframe. Two cafes will be added to encounter a growing number of visitors, whereas restaurants will be moving to the middle of the amusement park. Also remarkable is the fact that haunted houses will be included in 2035, where fans get to **experience terror and an adrenaline rush**.

根據消息來源，遊樂園將會經歷一系列的改變以迎合那些挑剔的愛好者。在 2035 年，五個主要的設施和入口處會維持在同樣的地點。引人注目的是廁所的地點已經從接近入口處移至時光機和摩天輪中間，而且是要收費的，這是史無前例的。從所提供的資訊，位於入口處左側的旋轉木馬在 2035 年時會被書店所取代。另一項會新增的設施是時光機，而愛好者可以體驗回到過去特定時間點的特效。兩個咖啡廳也會新增以迎合日益增加的參觀者，而餐廳將會移至遊樂園的中間處。值得注目的是在 2035 年會新增鬼屋，愛好者能夠體驗恐怖和腎上腺素分泌的激增。

Although Amusement Park will be having **moderate altercations**, it does contain the fundamental feature to every potential visitor. With addition of two cafes and so on, it will certainly elevate the experience.

儘管遊樂園將會有些微的改變，它仍包含對每個潛在拜訪者所需的基礎設施。隨著兩個咖啡廳的增加等，它確實能提升體驗。

UNIT 02 曲線圖題：棕熊族群數量因為天災產生的波動

Writing Task 1

You should spend about 20 minutes on this task

The diagram below shows the number of the brown bears from 1949 to 2019. The population encountered several fluctuations due to natural disasters. The statistics conducted here measures the number of brown bears per decade.

Summarize the information by selecting and reporting the main features, and make comparisons where relevant.

Write at least 150 words

整合能力強化 ❶ 實際演練

請搭配左頁的題目和下方的圖片進行圖表題寫作的演練。

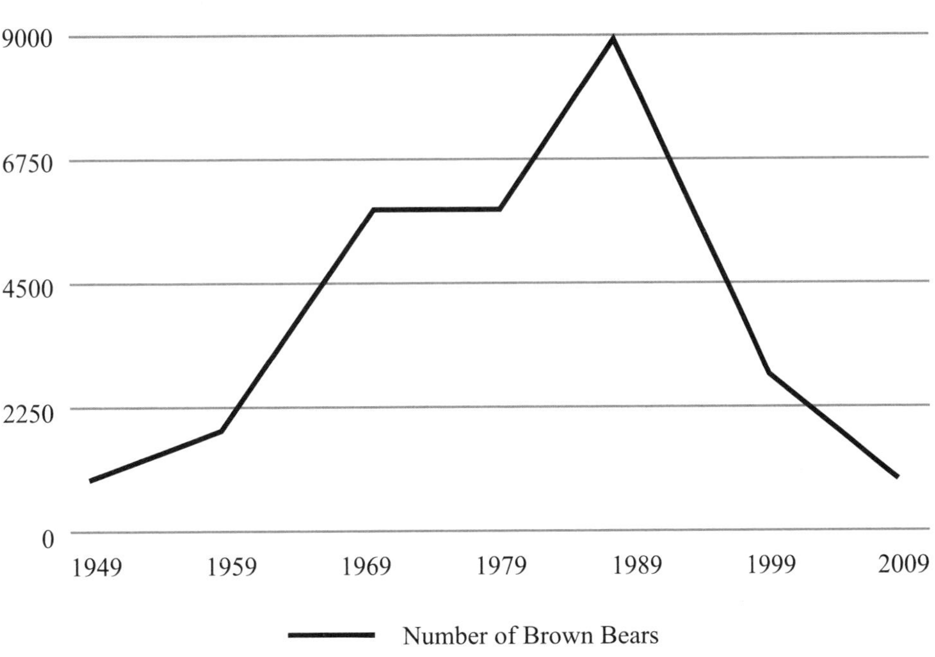

整合能力強化 ❷ 單句中譯英演練

❶ 從開始，於 1959 年有著些微的爬升來至 2000 隻。

【參考答案】

From the onset, there was a slight climb to two thousand in 1959.

❷ 然後，數量有了指數型的成長，於 1969 年時激增至 6000 隻，比起 1959 年有著急遽的增加。

【參考答案】

Then the number experienced exponential growth, ballooning to 6,000 in 1969, a dramatic increase from 1959.

❸ 而 10 年後，棕熊的數量達到高原期，而且持續到接下的 10 年。

【參考答案】

Then a decade later, the number of brown bears reached a plateau and even to the subsequent ten years.

❹ 在 1989 年，棕熊的總到達巔峰的 9000 隻，但是並未於接下來的年間維持不變。

____

____

【參考答案】
In 1989, the sum of brown bears pinnacled at 9,000, but did not remain constant over the year.

❺ 取而代之的是，在 1999 年棕熊數量重跌至僅剩 3000 隻，十年間驟降。

____

____

【參考答案】
Instead, the number of brown bears plummeted to only 3,000 in 1999, a dramatic decrease from the previous decade.

TOPIC

The diagram below shows the number of the brown bears from 1949 to 2019. The population encountered several fluctuations due to natural disasters. The statistics conducted here measures the number of brown bears per decade.

Summarize the information by selecting and reporting the main features, and make comparisons where relevant.

Step 1 先看題目的圖表題為何種形式，並統一以 **Given is/are... diagram(s)...** or **A glance at the graph(s)**.... 等套句開頭，避免使用 the pic shows... 等較低階的簡單句型。

- 在有年份的圖表題時，要避免每句開頭都是 in＋年份，這樣會顯得單調，所以次句以 from 1949 **onward** 為開頭。
- 使用更能體現圖表題的專業字彙像是 **fluctuation**，並加上高階形容詞 consecutive，表示是一接續的波動，另外在天災的描述部分換個字彙，catastrophes。
- 下一句以 It is **intriguing** to note... 為開頭，常見考生使用 it is interesting to note。若改用 intriguing 其實更好代表你知道這個較 interesting 高階的字彙。

■ 使用 went through **oscillation** 和 at a ten-year interval，代表族群經歷的擺動和圖表的年份是以 10 年為一個階段。接著描述族群的數量在最開頭和最尾端都是相同的數量，一千隻。

Step 2 接著也是避免使用 in＋年份為開頭，改使用 from the onset 為開頭，並描述 there was a slight climb...。接續以高分慣用語 **exponential growth** 描述族群的成長，並搭配高階動詞 **balloon**（激增）表達出數量在 1969 年達到 6000 隻。

Step 3 接續改以 Then a decade later 開頭，外加高分語彙 **reached a plateau**，表達族群進入高原期，且此情況接續到下個十年。開頭使用 in 1989，搭配用高階字彙 **pinnacle** 表達族群達到顛峰，以 but 表達轉折接續搭配高階慣用語 did not **remain constant**，最後接續以高階字彙 plummet 描述族群的下降，此句後搭配使用「同位語」表達這與前年是 a dramatic decrease，最後使用名詞 a mild **reduction** 表達些微的下降，最後用動詞的表達 **descend** 結束描述的部分。

Step 4 最後總結，使用 **succession** 和 natural **calamities** 豐富表達，最後陳述出族群數量在開頭跟結尾維持一致。

  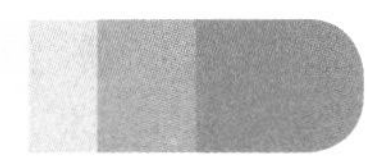

整合能力強化 ❹ 參考範文 ▶ *MP3 002*

經由先前的演練後，現在請看整篇範文並聆聽音檔

Given is a diagram illustrating the number of brown bears from 1949 to 2019. From 1949 **onward**, there has been a **consecutive** **fluctuation** due to the **severity** of the natural **catastrophes**. It is **intriguing** to note that after the same population went through **oscillation** at a ten-year interval, the number of brown bears remains the same to only a thousand in both 1949 and 2019.

提供的是一個圖表說明從 1949 年到 2019 年棕熊的數量。從 1949 年推進，由於天災的嚴重程度，棕熊的數量一直受到波動。引人注目的是在族群經歷過每隔十年為期的擺動，棕熊數量在 1949 年和 2019 年間維持不變，僅僅 1000 隻。

From the onset, there was a slight climb to two thousand in 1959. Then the number **experienced** **exponential** **growth**, **ballooning** to 6,000 in 1969, a dramatic increase from 1959. Then a decade later, the number of brown bears **reached a** **plateau** and even to the **subsequent** ten years. In 1989, the sum of brown bears **pinnacled** at 9,000, but did not **remain constant** over the year. Instead, the number of brown bears **plummeted** to only 3,000 in

1999, a **dramatic decrease** from the previous decade. The number of brown bears failed to recover to the initial state, and encountered **a mild reduction** to 2,000 in 2009. Ultimately, the number of brown bears **descends** to only a thousand.

開始於 1959 年時，棕熊的數量有著些微的爬升來至 2000 隻。然後，數量經歷了指數成長，於 1969 年激增至 6000 隻，這是從 1959 年以來的急遽增加。10 年之後，棕熊的數量達到高原期，甚至持續到接下的 10 年。在 1989 年時，棕熊的總數來到巔峰的 9000 隻，但是並未於接下來的年間維持不變。取而代之的是，在 1999 年時，棕熊的數量重跌至僅剩 3000 隻，與前一個 10 年相比是個急遽的跌幅。棕熊數量未能回復至先前的水平，而在 2009 年經歷些微的減少至 2000 隻。最終，棕熊的數量降至僅剩 1000 隻。

In conclusion, the number of brown bears, after 70 years of **succession** due to natural **calamities**, only **endures a thousand**, the same as the number at the very beginning. (209 words)

總結，在經歷了 70 年天災的影響所造成的消長，棕熊的數量僅只剩下 1000 隻，這個數量與最初相同。

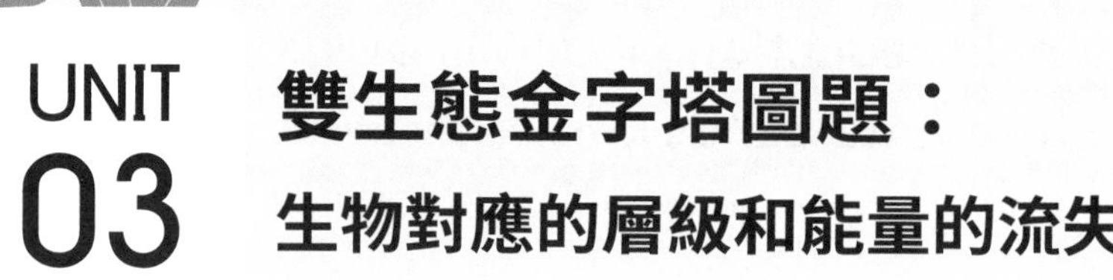

UNIT 03 雙生態金字塔圖題：生物對應的層級和能量的流失

Writing Task 1

You should spend about 20 minutes on this task

The diagram below includes two ecological pyramids, figure a and figure b. In figure a, you will find the representative of organisms in a specific layer. It is another realization of the concept of food chain or food web. In figure b, you will find that energy transferring from one to the next suffers energy loss, so only around 10% of the amount can be retained.

Summarize the information by selecting and reporting the main features, and make comparisons where relevant.

Write at least 150 words

整合能力強化 ❶ 實際演練

請搭配左頁的題目和下方的圖片進行圖表題寫作的演練。

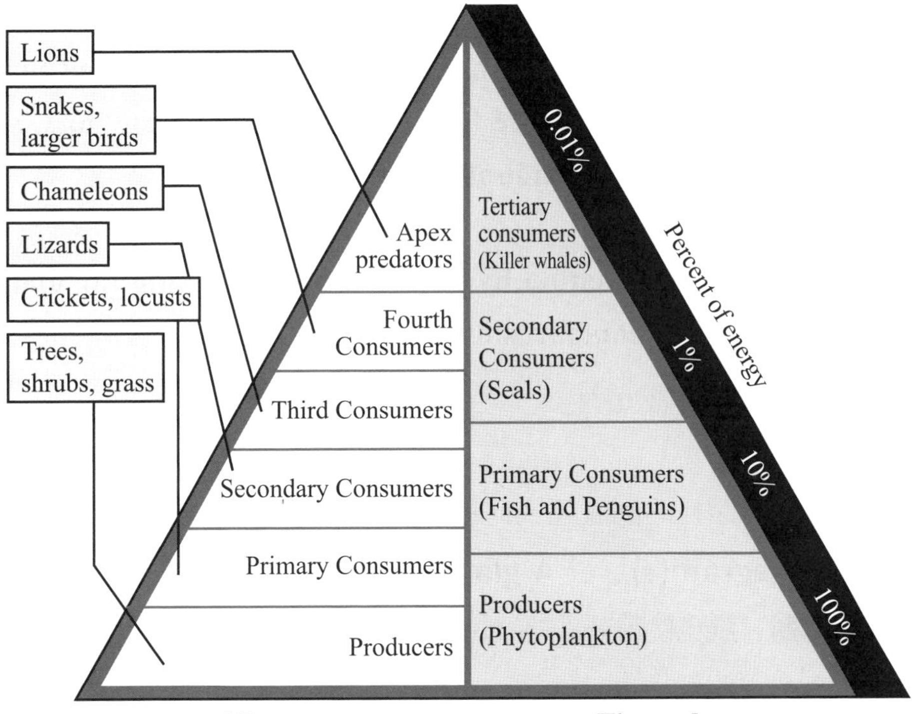

整合能力強化 ❸ 段落拓展

TOPIC

The diagram below includes two ecological pyramids, figure a and figure b. In figure a, you will find the representative of organisms in a specific layer. It is another realization of the concept of food chain or food web. In figure b, you will find that energy transferring from one to the next suffers energy loss, so only around 10% of the amount can be retained.

Summarize the information by selecting and reporting the main features, and make comparisons where relevant.

Step 1 先看題目的圖表題為何種形式，並統一以 **Given is/are**... **diagram(s)**... or **A glance at the graph(s)**.... 等套句開頭，避免使用 the pic shows…等較低階的簡單句句型。

Step 2 使用高階字 **hierarchy**，表達在 figure a 中區分成六個範疇，使用 ranging from A to B 的表達並於 A（producers）和 B（apex predators）後以形容詞子句補述（範文的底線部分），此舉可以增添句型 variety 的分數。

Step 3 接著使用 As can be seen from the graph 為開頭，接下來的描述要注意兩個增添句型組成變化和增加字彙使用分數的地方。

- 第一個是在表達「組成」的部分要熟悉 consist of 和 is made up of 等常見用法，避免一個句型用到底。在 producers 和 primary consumers 後面都用上不同的「組成」表達，並注意到 primary consumers 後省略了 **which are**。
- 另一個注意的點是使用高階字彙增添風采，primary consumer 就是 **herbivore**（接續慣用語後），而 secondary consumer 就是 **omnivore**（使用同位語加上這個字），還有後面的肉食性動物 **carnivore**，這都能提升語彙表達。還有在 third consumer 部分用上 **tertiary** 這個字。最後是避免直接使用金字塔的動物，換字改用 small insects 等取代。

Step 4 在 figure b 部分使用 **A glance at the graph(s)**.... 的套句開頭，接著 a more **simplified** version 表達跟 figure a 的差異處。接著使用 The **foundation** of..., the **subsequent** categories... 和 The pinnacle of…，並以形容詞子句表達補述 whales。然後使用 It is **intriguing** to note. 以及同位語 **a remarkable difference** from figure a.。然後可以參考範文中能量流失的描述，其實還有很多重點可以描述，例如比較頂端掠食者和生產者就可以描述僅能保留千分之一的能量。（考生可以多練習其它描述的句型）

Step 5 最後是總結這兩個圖表。

 整合能力強化 ❹ 參考範文 ▶ *MP3 003* 

經由先前的演練後，現在請看整篇範文並聆聽音檔

Given are two figures (figure a and figure b) about ecological pyramids. The **hierarchy** in figure a divides into six categories, ranging from producers, which are at the bottom, to apex predators, which occupy the highest rank. As can be seen from the graph, producers, **consist mostly of** trees, shrubs, and grass, and primary consumers, **largely made up of herbivores**, such as crickets and locusts feed on the producers for food. Secondary consumers, also **omnivores**, including lizards eat primary consumers. From the information supplied, the following two divisions are **tertiary** consumers and fourth consumers randomly eating small insects and omnivores from the previous rank. Finally, there are apex predators, also the **carnivores**, and the **representative** of the highest rank, such as lions, which have almost zero threats in the natural world.

提供的是兩個圖表（figure a 和 figure b）說明生態金字塔。在 figure a 的階層等級可以區分成六個範疇，範圍從位於底部的生產者到佔據最高階層的頂端掠食者。如圖片所示，生產者大部分是由樹木、灌木和草所組成，而主要消費者大部分是由草食性動物，例如蟋蟀和蝗蟲，以生產者為食的動物。次級消費者，也就是雜食性動物，包含蜥蜴，食用主要消費者。所提供的資訊中，接下來的兩個分層是第三級消費者和第四級消費者，隨機以先前層級中的小型昆蟲和雜食性動物為食。最後是頂端掠食者，也就是肉食性動物，最高層級的代表，例如獅子，在自然界中的威脅近乎是零。

A glance at the figure b provided reveals another aspect of the role of organisms in each hierarchy. Figure b demonstrates a more **simplified** version of the ecological pyramid, which only consists of four categories. The foundation of the ecological pyramid is phytoplankton, and the subsequent categories contain seals and "fish and penguins" respectively. The **pinnacle** of the pyramid is occupied by killer whales, which are apex predators in this ecosystem.

掃視圖表 b 所揭露在每個階層中生物有機體的另外一個面向。圖表 b 展示了生態金字塔的簡化版本，僅僅由四個範疇所組成。生態金字塔底部是浮游生物，而接續的範疇包含了海豹和「魚和企鵝」。金字塔頂端是由殺人鯨所佔據，也就是這個生態系統中的頂級掠食者。

It is **intriguing** to note that there is the percent of energy next to each layer, a remarkable difference from figure a. The producers get a hundred percent energy, but in the next layer, the energy is only 10% left. It is evident from the information provided that there is bound to be a 90 percent energy loss occurring from one layer to the next. The energy loss is unbelievably tremendous, leaving the tertiary animals, such killer whales, retained only **a thousandth** of the energy.

引人注意的是在每個層級旁有著能量的百分比，這點是跟圖表 a 有顯著不同之處。生產者獲得 100%的能量，但是到了下個階層，能量僅剩 10%。從提供的資訊可以明顯看出，從一個階層到下一個階層間有著 90%的能量流失。能量流失之大是令人難以置信的，這使得第三層級的動物，例如殺人鯨僅獲得千分之一的能量。

To sum up, both pyramids represent different concepts of biology, although some parts are correlated. The former one shows the role and relationships from each layer through the realization of the food web, and the latter one is about the energy loss and the scarcity of energy that retains.

總結，兩個金字塔代表著不同的生物學概念，儘管有些部分是相關聯的。前者展示出每個階層的角色和關係，透過食物網的概念來呈現，而後者是關於能量流失和能量稀有性的保存。

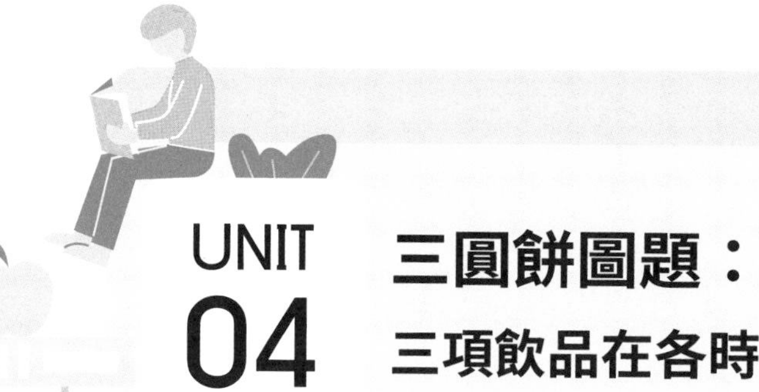

UNIT 04 三圓餅圖題：三項飲品在各時段的飲用比例

Writing Task 1

You should spend about 20 minutes on this task

The diagram below includes three pie charts. Each pie chart represents a major drink in Taiwan. The percentage of the consumption of three drinks in four major meals can actually reveal people's habits and preference for drinks in a specific timeframe.

Summarize the information by selecting and reporting the main features, and make comparisons where relevant.

Write at least 150 words

整合能力強化 ❶ 實際演練

請搭配左頁的題目和下方的圖片進行圖表題寫作的演練。

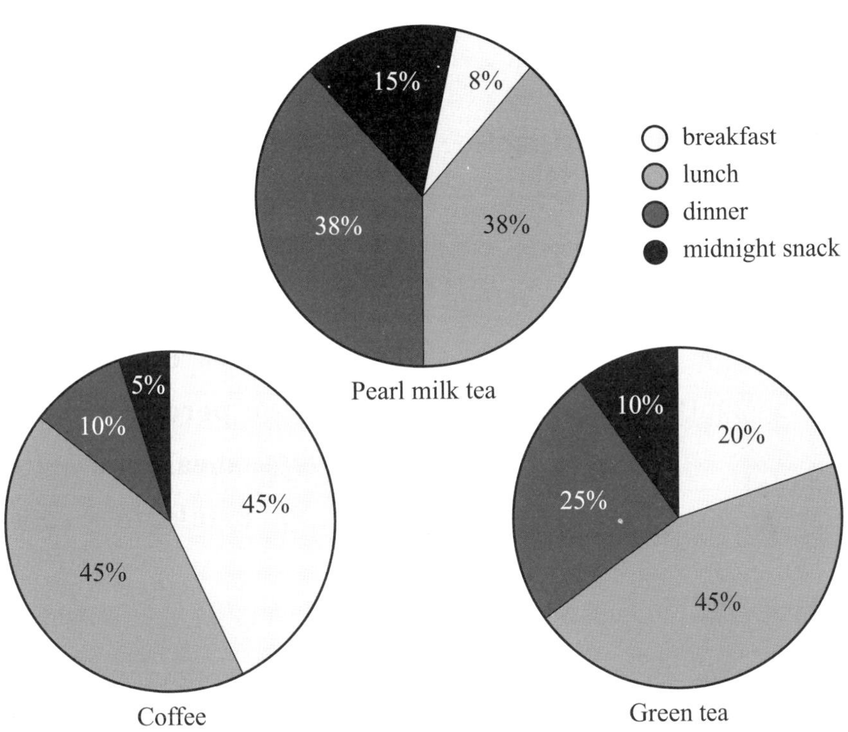

整合能力強化 ❷ 單句中譯英演練

❶ 在早餐期間，咖啡勝出，有著 45%的大比率，而綠茶有著最低的百分比，僅有 20%的比率。

【參考答案】

During the breakfast, coffee prevails, with a significant 45%, while green tea has the lowest percentage, consisting of only 20 percent.

❷ 引人注目的是在午餐期間，綠茶和咖啡均有著相同比率的消費型態，45%的比率。

【參考答案】

It is intriguing to note that during the lunch, green tea and coffee both have the same portion of consumption, 45%.

❸ 與珍珠奶茶相比較，在早餐期間飲用咖啡的比例比起飲用珍珠奶茶的比例更高。

【參考答案】
Compared with pearl milk tea, the percentage of coffee during the breakfast is immensely greater than that of pearl milk tea.

❹ 在珍珠奶茶的部分，午餐和晚餐有著同樣的消費情形，分別佔有39%和38%的比率。

____

____

【參考答案】
In the pearl milk tea section, lunch and dinner have identical consumption, respectively having 39% and 38%.

❺ 總之，三個圓餅圖顯示出不僅是數據的百分比，而且是習慣的表現，因為習慣讓一個人所從事的事物和飲用的飲料有著固定的形式。

____

____

【參考答案】
To sum up, three pie charts exhibit not only the percentage of figures, but also the habit, since the habit sets the pattern of the day people do and consume.

整合能力強化 ❸ 段落拓展

TOPIC

The diagram below includes three pie charts. Each pie chart represents a major drink in Taiwan. The percentage of the consumption of three drinks in four major meals can actually reveal people's habits and preference for drinks in a specific timeframe.

Summarize the information by selecting and reporting the main features, and make comparisons where relevant.

Step 1 先看題目的圖表題為何種形式，並統一以 Given is/are... diagram(s)... or A glance at the graph(s).... 等套句開頭，避免使用 the pic shows... 等較低階的簡單句型。

Step 2 很快掃描三個圓餅圖後開始構思，重點一定要放在比較相似處和相異處，避免只是一直陳述文句但缺少各個飲品或各飲用時間的比較，這樣分數不會高。

- 先以早餐期間為開頭比較了咖啡和綠茶，而咖啡有了 a **significant** 45%，這是個很好的比較開頭，接續使用了 It is intriguing to note，比較了午餐的部分，然後使用很常用

的比較慣用語 **compared with**，並使用了 is **immensely** greater than that of pearl milk tea。

- 最後在同個項目內比較了珍珠奶茶，用到了 **identical** consumption 和 **respectively** having 是很好的表達。

Step 3 次段落使用 **From the information supplied** 這個常見的切入句，在午夜餐點的部分進行比較，運用到了 **remarkably lower**，還有提到一個高階字 **caffeine** 和相關描述豐富了綠茶和咖啡的表達，最後提到在早晨的部分咖啡因扮演的重要角色。

Step 4 最後總結出，這也跟習慣有關，習慣影響一個人的消費行為。

整合能力強化 ❹ 參考範文 ▶ MP3 004

經由先前的演練後，現在請看整篇範文並聆聽音檔

A glance at three pie charts provided reveals the average consumption in different meals. During the breakfast, coffee prevails, with a **significant** 45%, while green tea has the lowest percentage, consisting of only 20 percent. It is intriguing to note that during lunch, green tea and coffee both have the same portion of consumption, 45%. **Compared with** pearl milk tea, the percentage of coffee during the breakfast is **immensely** greater than that of pearl milk tea. In the pearl milk tea section, lunch and dinner have **identical** consumption, **respectively** having 39% and 38%.

掃視所提供的三個圓餅圖揭露了不同餐點中的平均消費。在早餐期間，咖啡勝出，有著大比率的 45%，而綠茶有著最低的百分比，僅有 20%。引人注目的是在午餐期間，綠茶和咖啡均有著相同比例的消費情形，45%的比率。與珍珠奶茶相比較，在早餐期間飲用咖啡的比例比起飲用珍珠奶茶的比例更高。在珍珠奶茶的部分，午餐和晚餐有著同樣的消費情形，分別佔有 39%和 38%的比率。

From the information supplied, in the midnight snack section, coffee and green tea all have **remarkably lower** consumption in their component, perhaps due to the fact that they contain **caffeine**, which **invigorates** the brain, making people harder to fall asleep. In the morning; however, this is served as the important function so that people go to work with a coffee in hand.

從所提供的資訊中顯示，在午夜的宵夜部分，咖啡和綠茶在他們的組成部分，都有顯著低比例的消費情形，或許是由於他們包含咖啡因，能使大腦活耀，讓人們更難入睡。然而，在早晨，這卻被視為是重要的功能，如此人們去上班時手裡就有杯咖啡。

To sum up, three pie charts exhibit not only the percentage of figures, but also the habit, since **the habit sets the pattern of the day** people do and consume.

總之，三個圓餅圖顯示出的不僅是數據的百分比，而且是習慣的表現，因為習慣讓一個人所從事的事物和飲用的飲料有著固定的形式。

UNIT 05 柱狀圖題：四項小遊戲在三個不同年齡層的遊戲次數高低

Writing Task 1

You should spend about 20 minutes on this task

The diagram below includes four major small games people usually play in Taiwan.
The bar graph measures the frequency, how many times people play, and four major games in three different age groups.

Summarize the information by selecting and reporting the main features, and make comparisons where relevant.

Write at least 150 words

整合能力強化 ❶ 實際演練

請搭配左頁的題目和下方的圖片進行圖表題寫作的演練。

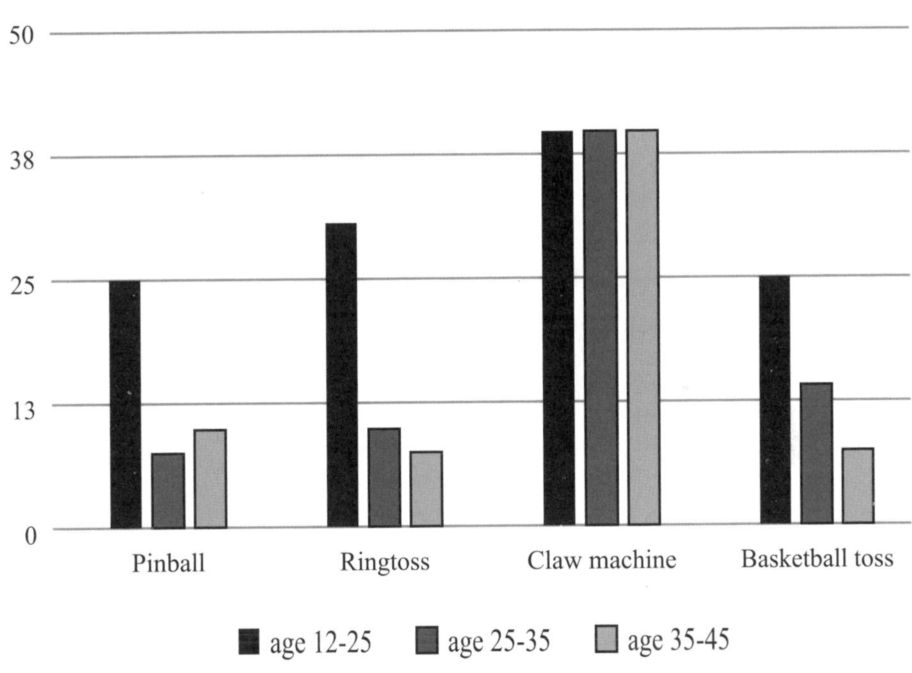

整合能力強化 ❷ 單句中譯英演練

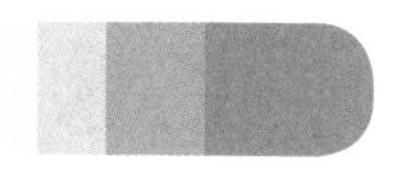

在掌握文法句型後，學習者大多能拿到 7 分以上的寫作成績，英語句型多樣性和各式句型是獲取高分的關鍵，現在請演練接下來的單句中譯英練習。請務必演練後再觀看答案，並於觀看答案後仔細聆聽音檔，強化對各句型的記憶。

❶ 從所提供的資料顯示，夾娃娃機在三個不同的年齡層中有著相同的遊戲次數，而其他三個小遊戲，遊戲次數則不同且有波動。

____

____

【參考答案】

From the information supplied, claw machines have the same frequency of playing, 40 times in three various age groups, whereas in other three small games, the frequency of playing varies and fluctuates.

❷ 在彈珠球遊戲中，12-25 歲遊戲次數為 25 次，但是到了 25-35 歲時有著顯著的跌幅，僅剩下 5 次，然後在 35-45 歲時有些微爬升至 10 次。

____

____

【參考答案】

In pinballs, the frequency of playing in age 12-25 has 25 times, but drops significantly to only 5 times in age 25-35, then climbing slightly to 10 times in age 35-45.

❸ 在丟圈圈中，較年輕的世代即 12-25 歲的年齡層中有著最高的遊戲次數，而到了 25-35 歲的年齡層則有了顯著的跌幅來到 10 次，在 35-45 歲的年齡層中有著逐步的降幅。

【參考答案】
In ring tosses, the frequency of playing also has the highest among younger groups, in age 12-25, and has an immense descend to 10 times in age 25-35, followed by a gradual decrease in age 35-45.

❹ 引人注目的是在籃球投擲，在較年長的世代中有著最低比率的遊戲次數。

【參考答案】
It is intriguing to note that in basketball tosses, the frequency of playing also has the lowest rates of playing among older generations.

❺ 人們越年長，越少人玩籃球投擲的小遊戲，因為它需要體力。

【參考答案】
The older people get, the less people play basketball toss, a game that requires physical stamina.

整合能力強化 ❸ 段落拓展

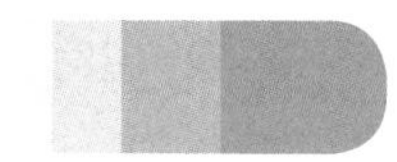

TOPIC

The diagram below includes four major small games people usually play in Taiwan.

The bar graph measures the frequency, how many times people play, and four major games in three different age groups.

Summarize the information by selecting and reporting the main features, and make comparisons where relevant.

Step 1 先看題目的圖表題為何種形式，並統一以 Given is/are... diagram(s)... or A glance at the graph(s).... 等套句開頭，避免使用 the pic shows... 等較低階的簡單句型。

Step 2 接著看下圖表中有四個小遊戲、玩遊戲的次數和三個主要年齡層，然後開始構思，重點一樣放在比較異同處，使用切入句 **From the information supplied**，先看娃娃機的部分和其他三項小遊戲的比較，並運用到兩個關鍵動詞 varies and **fluctuates**。

Step 3 依序看玩彈珠、套圈圈和投籃球的部分。玩彈珠用到了 has 25 times, but **drops significantly** to only 5 times in age 25-35, then **climbing slightly** to 10 times in age 35-45.（很流暢的表達可以記下來）。在套圈圈的部分則用到 **an immense descend** to 10 times in age 25-35, followed by **a gradual decrease** in age 35-45.。（要注意時態和形容詞子句的省略）。最後以 It is **intriguing** to note 表達投籃球的部分，描述到人們越年長越缺乏精力在這個小遊戲上。

Step 4 最後以娃娃機的部分總結，提到了娃娃機的流行度和跨年齡層的受歡迎程度，用到了 **transcends** all three age groups, **remaining remarkably constant**，可以將這些用法記下。

整合能力強化 4 參考範文 ▶ MP3 005

經由先前的演練後，現在請看整篇範文並聆聽音檔

Given is a diagram about four major small games people play in Taiwan and with three different age groups. **From the information supplied**, claw machines have the same frequency of playing, 40 times in three various age groups, whereas in other three small games, the frequency of playing varies and **fluctuates**. In pinballs, the frequency of playing in age 12-25 has 25 times, but **drops significantly** to only 5 times in age 25-35, then **climbing slightly** to 10 times in age 35-45. In ring tosses, the frequency of playing also has the highest among younger groups, in age 12-25, and has **an immense descend** to 10 times in age 25-35, followed by **a gradual decrease** in age 35-45. It is **intriguing** to note that in basketball tosses, the frequency of playing also has the lowest rates of playing among older generations. **Since basketball toss is a game that requires physical stamina, the older people get, the less people play basketball toss.**

提供的是一個圖表說明人們在台灣玩的四個主要的小遊戲且區分成三個年齡組成。從所提供的資料顯示，夾娃娃機在三個不同的年齡層中有著相同的遊戲次數，而在其他三個小遊戲，遊戲次數則不同且有波動。在彈珠球遊戲中，12-25 歲的遊戲次數為 25 次，但是到了 25-35 歲時有著顯著的跌幅，僅剩下 5 次，在 35-45 歲時，些微爬升至 10 次。在丟圈圈中，較年輕的世代即 12-25 歲的年齡層中有著最高的遊戲次數，而到了 25-35 歲的年齡層有了顯著的跌幅來到 10 次，接續在 35-45 歲的年齡層中有著逐步的降幅。引人注目的是在籃球投擲，較年長的世代中有著最低比率的遊戲次數。人們越年長，越少人玩籃球投擲的小遊戲，因為其需要身體的精力。

In conclusion, the claw machine **transcends** all three age groups, **remaining remarkably constant** in the number of times people play, 40 times. The popularity of the claw machine makes it a game not only suitable for all age groups, but also **triumphs** the other three small games.

總之，娃娃機跨越了三個年齡層，驚人地維持在人們玩小遊戲的次數 40 次。娃娃機的流行程度讓它不僅僅適於所有年齡層，而且在其他三個小遊戲中拔得頭籌。

UNIT 06 流程圖題：湖泊消長的四個階段圖

Writing Task 1

You should spend about 20 minutes on this task

The diagram below shows four stages of the lake. From the beginning of the lake, figure a to figure d, after encountering the succession. The lake goes through processes (A-D) and eventually has become a static, nonfluid, dead lake.

Summarize the information by selecting and reporting the main features, and make comparisons where relevant.

Write at least 150 words

整合能力強化 ❶ 實際演練

請搭配左頁的題目和下方的圖片進行圖表題寫作的演練。

Aquatic Succession

Lake A

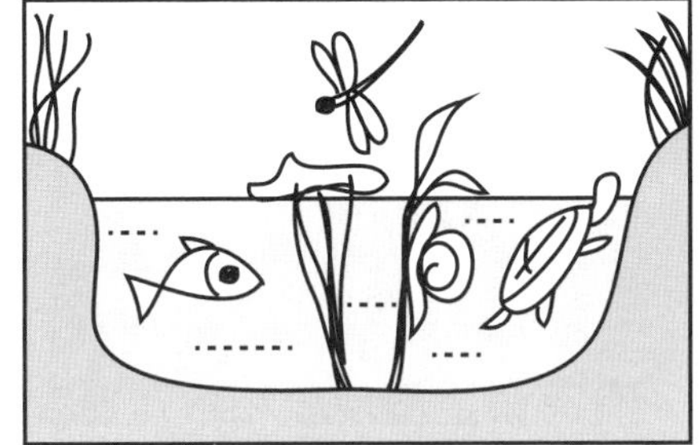

Lake B

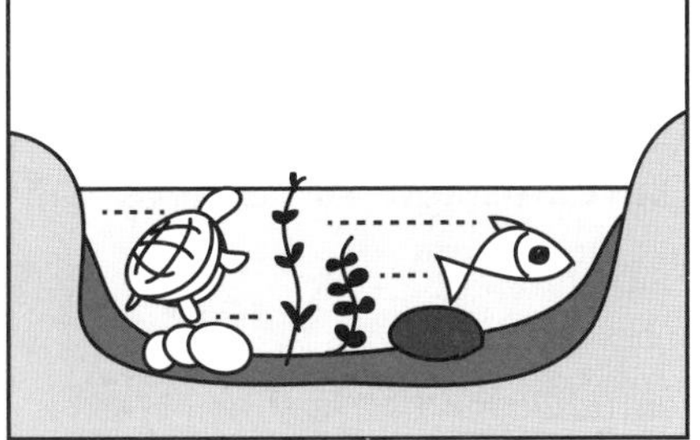

Lake C

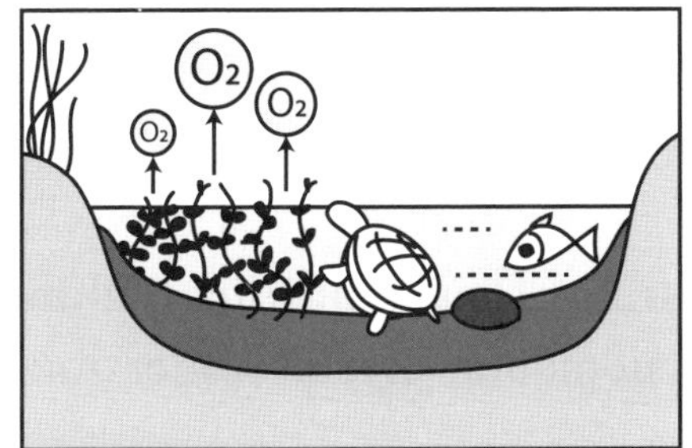

Lake D

整合能力強化 ❷ 單句中譯英演練

❶ 湖泊是短暫的，而大多數的時候它們會經歷幾個階段的變化而死亡。

____

____

【參考答案】

Lakes are ephemeral, and most of the time they will go through several stages of changes and die.

❷ 湖泊演進的過程就稱為湖泊消長。有時候這個現象和水質優養化有關。

____

____

【參考答案】

The processes of the progression of a lake are called lake succession. Sometimes the phenomenon of eutrophication is involved.

❸ 雨量沖刷掉土地上的沉積物和營養物質。這些物質最終儲藏到湖泊裡。

____

____

【參考答案】

Rainfall washes away sediments and nutrients from the land. These materials eventually stash into the lake.

❹ 沉降的物質對於水生植物，例如藻類是個恩賜。

【參考答案】

Submerging materials are a boon to water plants, such algae.

❺ 隨著時間的演進，沉積物使得湖泊的整體大小縮水了，而在湖泊中逐漸滋長的營養物質讓藻類繁盛。

【參考答案】

Throughout the passage of time, sediments make the overall size of the lake shrink, whereas growing nutrients in the lake make algae groom.

TOPIC

The diagram below shows four stages of the lake. From the beginning of the lake, figure a to figure d, after encountering the succession. The lake goes through processes (A-D) and eventually has become a static, nonfluid, dead lake.

Summarize the information by selecting and reporting the main features, and make comparisons where relevant.

Step 1 先看題目的圖表題為何種形式，並統一以 **Given is/are... diagram(s)**... or **A glance at the graph(s)**.... 等套句開頭，避免使用 the pic shows... 等較低階的簡單句型。

Step 2 先看一下圖形的變化，這題較難，可以想下湖泊的變化，運用到短暫的高階形容詞 **ephemeral**。**定義**並表達出這個現象水質優養化有關。The processes of the **progression** of a lake are called lake **succession**. Sometimes the phenomenon of **eutrophication** is involved.

Step 3 接著描述起初湖泊的狀態到變化的部分，用到了 remains **impervious** to 和幾個高階字 **sediments** and **nutrients, stash** 和 **Submerging**。最後提到關鍵的物質水藻。

Step 4 接續構思湖泊接續可能面臨到的變化，幾個變化都導致湖泊的面積又萎縮了，當中運用到幾個高階字 make algae **groom, proportion**, **oxygen**, **living organisms**。然後要想到湖泊漸漸由原先狀態變成沼澤狀態到更加萎縮的狀態，最後面臨死亡。大概主要的變化點都描述到其實就差不多了，可以多注意這類的考題，不會突然遇到時一時之間不知道要怎麼應對。

整合能力強化 ❹ 參考範文 ▶ *MP3 006*

經由先前的演練後，現在請看整篇範文並聆聽音檔

Given is a diagram about the succession of a lake. Lakes are **ephemeral**, and most of the time they will go through several stages of changes and die. The processes of the **progression** of a lake are called lake **succession**. Sometimes the phenomenon of **eutrophication** is involved.

提供的是一個圖表說明湖泊的消長。湖泊是短暫的，而大多數的時候它們會經歷幾個階段的變化而死亡。湖泊演進的過程就稱為湖泊消長。有時候這個現象和水質優養化有關。

Originally, the lake remains **impervious** to the change and is pretty healthy.（Lake A）Rainfall washes away **sediments** and **nutrients** from the land. These materials eventually **stash** into the lake. **Submerging** materials are a boon to water plants, such algae.

起初，湖泊對於改變不為所動而且相當健康。（**湖泊** A）雨量沖刷土地上的沉積物和營養物質。這些物質最終儲藏到湖泊裡。沉降的物質對於水生植物，例如藻類是個恩賜。

Throughout the passage of time, sediments make the overall size of the lake shrink, whereas growing nutrients in the lake make algae **groom**. The **proportion** of the lake gets even smaller.（Lake B）Reeds and grass around the lake also build up. Other species of trees and plants also **take up** the space of the lake. In addition, **algae boom deprives of** the **oxygen** in the lake, making **living organisms** harder to live.（Lake C）The lake initially a **wetland** has become a dead one later, with fewer species living and the space shrinking. Ultimately, more sediments **fill in** the lake and the lake dies.（Lake D） It has become a land that we see later.

隨著時間的演進，沉積物使得湖泊的整體大小縮水了，而在湖泊中逐漸滋長的營養物質讓藻類繁盛。湖泊的比例甚至變得更小了。**（湖泊 B）**湖邊的蘆葦和草也建構起來。其他種類的樹木和植物也佔據著湖泊的空間。此外，藻類的繁盛剝奪了湖泊中的氧氣，讓活著的有機體更難生存。**（湖泊 C）**湖泊起初是個沼澤，隨著生存的物種更少且空間縮小，於稍後已經變成死亡湖泊。最終，更多的沉積物填入湖泊裡頭，以至於湖泊死亡了。**（湖泊 D）**這已經成為了我們稍後看到的土地了。

UNIT 07 流程圖題：韓式泡菜製作流程

Writing Task 1

You should spend about 20 minutes on this task

The diagram below includes seven procedures about making the simple Korean kimchi. Describe these procedures in order and make them easily understandable.

The sequence is the key. Using these graphs while composing the article. You can add your knowledge about the dish to make it more appealing.

Write at least 150 words

整合能力強化 ❶ 實際演練

請搭配左頁的題目和下方的圖片進行圖表題寫作的演練。

1

2

3

4

5

6

7

Procedures Of
Making The Simple
Korean Kimchi

整合能力強化 ❷ 單句中譯英演練

❶ 製作這道享譽盛名的菜餚包含了七個步驟。

【參考答案】

Seven steps are included for making this prestigious dish.

❷ Salt is the key in the fermentation of the cabbage and sprinkle salt onto the cabbage leaves equally.

【參考答案】

鹽是大白菜發酵的關鍵，必將鹽均勻灑在白菜葉上。

❸ 第四個步驟是移除這些葉子上的鹽份，使得大白菜能維持無鹽且可供食用。

【參考答案】

The fourth step is about removal of salt on these leaves and the cabbage can remain not salty and edible.

④ 這些成分是由紅辣椒、洋蔥、大蒜和魚露所組成的。

【參考答案】
These ingredients are made up of red pepper, an onion, garlic, and fish sauce.

⑤ 將糊均勻分布在大白菜葉子上直到葉子都浸泡出風味。

【參考答案】
Spreading the paste evenly onto the cabbage leaves until they are soaked with flavor.

整合能力強化 ❸ 段落拓展

TOPIC

The diagram below includes seven procedures about making the simple Korean kimchi. Describe these procedures in order and make them easily understandable.

The sequence is the key. Using these graphs while composing the article. You can add your knowledge about the dish to make it more appealing.

Step 1 先看題目的圖表題為何種形式，並統一以 **Given is/are**... **diagram(s)**... 或 **A glance at the graph(s)**.... 等套句開頭，避免使用 the pic shows... 等較低階的簡單句型。

Step 2 可以增添一些變化，不一定要照 listing patterns 描述（即第一步驟到第七步驟），例如在段落中有使用到 **the next step**... 和 **final step**... 都是另一種替換。

Step 3 另一部分是，如作文中也有提到的就是使用你對於這道菜餚的知識，增進表達。在首段就包含了煮菜經驗的部分並適時融入步驟中，像是在描述將大白菜分成四等分的時

候，加入了不是用刀子切成四等分，而是在頭部切一小截後再撕成四等分，這也比較是韓國的作菜方式。另外還包含了像是以重物壓在大白菜上和適時的加上字，讓整體表達不會淪為生硬的作菜程序，可讀性可以更高。

Step 4 最後要提到的是句型變化，像這類的流程題目有很多，包含布或塑膠製成等，這類試題更難使用直條圖等的高階字彙去馬上描述出數值以獲取高分，加上不太好答，很可能看到題目就慌了。但是可以適時運用其他的句型而非簡單句型，讓作文更出色。例如可以使用動名詞當主詞的句型或是 To＋V..., S＋V...等等的句型或是 before 或 after 的句型調整步驟順序，讓整體作文表達跟其他人不一樣，考生也可以自己試試看，組織出不一樣的範文。

整合能力強化 ❹ 參考範文 ▶ MP3 007

經由先前的演練後，現在請看整篇範文並聆聽音檔

Given are diagrams about the procedures of making the simple Korean kimchi. Seven steps are included for making this prestigious dish. The first step involves evenly dividing the cabbage into quarters. It is advisable to cut the head for about an inch and split it into four parts by using hands, instead of using a knife. Salt is the key in the fermentation of the cabbage and sprinkle salt onto the cabbage leaves equally.

提供的圖表是關於製作簡易韓國泡菜的流程。製作這道享譽盛名的菜餚包含了七個步驟。第一個步驟是將大白菜均分成四等分。將大白菜頭切成約一寸並用手，而非使用刀子將其分成四份是更適當的方法。鹽是大白菜發酵的關鍵，並且將鹽均勻灑在白菜葉上。

The next step involves facilitation of the cabbage fermentation, so putting the heavy stuff onto the cabbage makes the fermentation rapider than letting it in a standstill. The fourth step is about removal of salt on these leaves and the cabbage can remain not salty and edible. To make it more palatable, ingredients are very important. These ingredients are made up of red pepper, an onion, garlic, and fish sauce. Using the blender to grind will make the paste smoother. Then comes the sixth step. Spreading the paste evenly onto the cabbage leaves until they are soaked with flavor. The final step will be putting the cabbage in the container in the refrigerator. After a week's magic fermentation, you will get the desired cabbage you want.

下一個步驟包含促成大白菜的發酵，所以要將重物壓在大白菜上，讓發酵更為快速，而非將其靜置。第四個步驟是移除這些葉子上的鹽份，使得大白菜能維持無鹽分且可供食用。為了讓其更為美味，原料也非常重要。這些成分是由紅辣椒、洋蔥、大蒜和魚露所組成的。使用攪拌機研磨會讓混合的糊更為順口。接著就是第六個步驟。將糊均勻分布在大白菜葉子上直到葉子都浸泡出風味。最後一個步驟是將大白菜放置在容器中並放入冰箱裡。在一個星期的魔力發酵後，你會得到你所想要的理想大白菜。

UNIT 01 對於承擔「風險」每個人的看法大相逕庭。而你對權衡風險的看法又是如何呢？

Writing Task 2

TOPIC

Some proclaim that risk is their middle name, and they are willing to do a greater risk than others to achieve certain goals. Others are chickened out, and they are afraid of doing any risk. Yet there are some who try to weigh the risk in order to accomplish a great result? What is your viewpoint? Use specific examples to back up your viewpoints.

Write at least 250 words

整合能力強化 ❶ 實際演練

請搭配左頁的題目和並構思和完成大作文的演練。

整合能力強化 ❷ 單句中譯英演練

❶ 這個所提出的觀念實際上也與阿諾德．唐納德，嘉年華的執行長，所給予的建議相吻合。

【參考答案】

The notion putting forward actually corresponds to the suggestion given by Arnold Donald, the world's largest cruise company's CEO.

❷ 兩者的觀念都與如何權衡風險以獲取更佳的成功率以及如何辨識出大學文憑的價值一直息息相關。

【參考答案】

Both concepts have been linked to how to weigh the risk for the greater probability of success and how to discern the value of a college diploma.

❸ 既然那是我們的主題，在這份寫作中，我僅會著重在討論前者。

【參考答案】

In the writing, I will exclusively accentuate on the former, since it is our main topic.

❹ 在《為什麼最便宜的機票不要買？：經濟學家教你降低生活中每件事的風險，做出最好的選擇》，當提及權衡幾個生活面向中的風險時，對大多數 20 歲的人來說，阿諾德・唐納德能充當為可作為楷模的例子。

____

____

【參考答案】

In *An Economist Walks into a Brothel: And Other Unexpected Places to Understand Risk*, Arnold Donald, the CEO of Carnival can be served as an exemplary example for most twentysomethings when it comes to weighing the risk in several aspects of their lives.

❺ 冒風險的同時亦傾向於能獲取更佳的成功結果是較好的選擇。

____

____

【參考答案】

Taking the risk while leaning towards the greater probability of success is a better option.

❻ 這也符合了其他暢銷書所提出的觀點，也就是你必須要思考的是「魚和熊掌兼得」。

【參考答案】

That also corresponds to the idea given by other bestsellers that you have to think both A and B.

❼ 阿諾德・唐納德設法在兩間大學裡分別獲取學位。

【參考答案】

Arnold Donald managed to have the study in both universities to have two separate degrees.

❽ 這使他獨樹一格和其餘的同袍有所區隔，而且史丹佛大學願意在唐納德於卡爾頓大學的經濟學系深造時保留他的獎學金。

【參考答案】

That separated him from the rest of his counterparts, and Sandford University would like to keep the scholarship while waiting for him to pursue economics at Carleton.

❾ 而且，他在稍後改選擇於華盛頓大學就讀，而非承受有學貸的財政風險（因為他的老婆並未獲得史丹佛大學的獎學金），如此一來，他們於畢業之後就不會負債。

____

____

【參考答案】
Also, instead of taking the financial risk of the student loan (because his wife didn't have the Sandford scholarship), he later chose to attend Washington University, so they will not have the debt after they graduate.

❿ 在職涯方面，他也構思出了其他方法。

____

____

【參考答案】
In career, he also had come up with other ways.

 整合能力強化 ❸ 段落拓展 

TOPIC

Some proclaim that risk is their middle name, and they are willing to do a greater risk than others to achieve certain goals. Others are chickened out, and they are afraid of doing any risk. Yet there are some who try to weigh the risk in order to accomplish a great result? What is your viewpoint? Use specific examples to back up your viewpoints.

搭配的暢銷書

- *The Personal MBA 10th Anniversary Edition*《不花錢讀名校 MBA（第 10 版周年紀念版）》
- *An Economist Walks into a Brothel*：*And Other Unexpected Places to Understand Risk*《為什麼最便宜的機票不要買？：經濟學家教你降低生活中每件事的風險，做出最好的選擇》

Step 1 首段先由暢銷書觀點切入主題，而非改寫或重述題目。由暢銷書觀點可以得到投報率的多寡，進而引出與另一本暢銷書觀點吻合的陳述。最後，才拉回正題，也就是要如何權衡風險。

Step 2 次段使用暢銷書實例，「冒風險的同時亦傾向於能獲取更佳的成功結果是較好的選擇。」得到權衡風險的折衷辦法。在進一步說明要如何「魚和熊掌兼得」。分別在兩所學校得到所具備的知識。

Step 3 在風險權衡中，捨棄名校思維，因為在不提供獎學金的前提下，會讓自己畢業後就有負債的風險。

Step 4 **運用 hedging 這個概念**，但也指出了「降低風險增加了你能夠獲取想要的結果的成功機率，但是你必須要放棄掉能得到更好結果的可能。」

Step 5 簡短的總結。

 整合能力強化 ❹ 參考範文 ▸ *MP3 008* 

經由先前的演練後，現在請看整篇範文並聆聽音檔

In *The Personal MBA 10th Anniversary Edition*, the author gives the advice of not pursuing an MBA degree offered by prestigious universities because the ROI (Return on Investment) is minus US 53,000 dollars. The notion putting forward actually corresponds to the suggestion given by Arnold Donald, the world's largest cruise company's CEO. Both concepts have been linked to how to weigh the risk for the greater probability of success and how to discern the value of a college diploma. In the writing, I will exclusively accentuate on the former, since it is our main topic.

在《不花錢讀名校 MBA（第 10 版周年紀念版）》中，作者給予了不要追求享譽盛名大學所提供的 MBA 學位，因為投資報酬是「負」五萬三千美元。這個所提出的觀念實際上也與阿諾德．唐納德，嘉年華的執行長，所給予的建議相吻合。兩者的觀念都與如何權衡風險以獲取更佳的成功率以及如何辨識出大學文憑的價值一直息息相關。既然這是我們的主題，在這份寫作中，我僅會著重在討論前者。

In *An Economist Walks into a Brothel：And Other Unexpected Places to Understand Risk*, Arnold Donald, the CEO of Carnival can be served as an exemplary example for most twentysomethings when it comes to weighing the risk in several aspects of their lives. Taking the risk while leaning towards the greater probability of success is a better option. That also corresponds to the idea given by other bestsellers that you have to think both A and B. Arnold Donald managed to have the study in both universities to have two separate degrees. That separated him from the rest of his counterparts, and Sandford University would like to keep the scholarship while waiting for him to pursue economics at Carleton. Also, instead of taking the financial risk of the student loan (because his wife didn't have the Sandford scholarship), he later chose to attend Washington University, so they will not have the debt after they graduate. In career, he also had come up with other ways.

在《為什麼最便宜的機票不要買？：經濟學家教你降低生活中每件事的風險，做出最好的選擇》，當提及權衡幾個生活面向中的風險時，對大多數 20 歲的人來說，阿諾德・唐納德能充當為可作為楷模的例子。冒風險的同時亦傾向於能獲取更佳的成功結果是較好的選擇。這也符合了其他暢銷書所提出的觀點，也就是你必須要思考的是「魚和熊掌兼得」。阿諾德・唐納德設法在兩間大學裡分別獲取學位。這使他獨樹一格和其餘的同袍有所區隔，而且史丹佛大學願意在唐納德於卡爾頓大學的經濟學系深造時保留他的獎學金。而且，他在稍後改選擇於華盛頓大學就讀，而非承受有學貸的財政風險（因為他的老婆並未獲得史丹佛大學的獎學金），如此一來，他們於畢業之後就不會負債。在職涯方面，他也構思出了其他方法。

His success rested on the concept of “hedging”. Hedging means de-risking or taking less risk. “de-risking increases the odds of getting what you want, but you must give up the probability of getting more.”

他的成功是仰賴 hedging 這個概念。Hedging 意謂著降低風險或承擔著較少的風險。「降低風險增加了你能夠獲取想要的結果的成功機率，但是你必須要放棄掉能得到更好結果的可能。」

To sum up, this has offered the neutral way for someone to succeed without taking too much risk. In life, we all have to learn how to weigh the risk in both our personal and professional life.

總之，這已經提供了獲取成功但是不需要承擔較多風險的中間法門。在生活中，我們都必須學習於我們的個人和專業生活中如何權衡當中的風險。

UNIT 02

「Digital natives」是個名詞用於形容的一直都與數位科技有所互動的使用者。現今，智慧型手機的普遍除了造成健康問題，也影響孩童學習，甚至手機被指為是孩童學習的最大阻礙，你同意這個看法嗎？

Writing Task 2

TOPIC

Digital natives are the term used to describe people who have been interacting with technologies, such as smartphones, and the phenomenon has resulted in a worrisome problem for most educators and parents. Other than health aspects, most students' learning has been heavily influenced by smartphones. Smartphones are said to be the greatest hindrance to children's learning? Do you agree? Do you have any solutions?

Write at least 250 words

整合能力強化 ❶ 實際演練

請搭配左頁的題目和並構思和完成大作文的演練。

整合能力強化 ❷ 單句中譯英演練

❶ 除了長期觀看智慧型手機會造成眼睛疲勞和頭痛之外，智慧型手機確實會讓小孩在學術研讀中更為分心。

【參考答案】

Aside from the fact that prolonged viewing on the smartphone does cause eyestrain and headaches, smartphones do make children more distracted in their academic study.

❷ 這項陳述讓今日的家長們憂心忡忡，因為他們的孩子一直都與數位科技有所互動。

【參考答案】

The statement would make today's parents increasingly worrisome, since their kids all have been interacting with digital technologies.

❸ 隨著他們很大程度地仰賴訊息容易吸收的短視頻和較為簡短的電子內容，這大幅地影響了孩子們的學習方式。

【參考答案】
This has greatly influenced children's ways of learning, as they rely heavily on short videos and shorter E-contents that are easily grasped.

❹ 在高中和大學求學期間，必需具備能瀏覽較長的文字的內容，對他們來說似乎是鑽火得冰。這會導致閱讀表現不佳，以及缺乏足夠的字彙以清楚表達自我。

____

____

【參考答案】
Navigation on longer texts, which are required during kids' academic studies in both high schools and colleges, may seem unlikely. This can result in a poor performance in reading, and a lack of enough vocabularies to express ourselves clearly.

❺ 研究發現，具有在讀書間坐下閱讀習慣的家庭，即使僅僅只有花費每天一小時的時間，對於小孩的學習有顯著的提升。

____

____

【參考答案】
Studies have found that families who customarily sit in a study room reading, even for just an hour a day, have a significant boost to children's learning.

❻ 不使用手機可能就是關鍵所在，而要讓這個絕佳的習慣成形或許是另一個促成的因素。

____

____

【參考答案】

Not using the phone is probably the key, and for the great habit to take hold is perhaps another contributor.

❼ 孩童必定會在終其一生都帶著這樣的好習慣，因此，對於他們之後的生活也會有極大的影響。

____

____

【參考答案】

Children are bound to take the good habit with them throughout their lives, thus, having a tremendous influence on their later lives.

❽ 養成好習慣似乎是現今父母們在不知道要如何教育子女時的解方。讓孩子們了解到遠離智慧型手機幾個小時對他們來說實際上是有益的。

____

____

【參考答案】

Good habit formation seems to be the cure for today's parents, who have no idea how to teach their kids. Making kids understood that a few hours away from the smartphones will actually do them good.

❾ 在讀書間一起讀書只是一個舉例。幾個小時的戶外活動或是演奏音樂樂器也能奏效。

【參考答案】

Reading together in a study room is just an example. A few hours of outdoor activities or playing music instrument can also work.

❿ 採用這個方法的家長們也會很快就會對於小孩日趨嚴重的視力不良和學校成績不佳的問題感到如釋重負。

【參考答案】

Parents adopting this method will soon find themselves relieved of kid's increasingly poor eyesight and bad school report cards.

整合能力強化 ❸ 段落拓展

TOPIC

Digital natives are the term used to describe people who have been interacting with technologies, such as smartphones, and the phenomenon has resulted in a worrisome problem for most educators and parents. Other than health aspects, most students' learning has been heavily influenced by smartphones. Smartphones are said to be the greatest hindrance to children's learning? Do you agree? Do you have any solutions?

Step 1

- 先由智慧型手機會造成小孩健康方面的影響（會造成眼睛疲勞和頭痛）切入主題。而且，會讓小孩在學習上無法專注。
- 再來，指出現今孩童「一直都與數位科技有所互動」，也就是從出生開始就開始接觸科技產品，所以他們「仰賴訊息容易吸收的短視頻和較為簡短敘述的電子內容」。
- 最後，推論出「影響孩童閱讀能力和有足夠的字彙以表達自我」。

Step 2

- 次段，由「研究發現」切入核心，直指有閱讀習慣的家庭，孩童的學術表現較為優異。另一個重點是，這讓他們不 24 小時仰賴手機，而是有固定的習慣，像閱讀，一天之中分散掉了一直檢視手機訊息的時間。
- 並進一步說明「孩童必定會在終其一生都帶著這樣的好習慣，因此，對於他們之後的生活也會有極大的影響。」以及「養成好習慣似乎是現今父母們在不知道要如何教育子女時的解方。」
- 從閱讀習慣作延伸，表達出有其他定期的才藝或戶外活動，並養成習慣，對小孩來說也是很大的助益。
- 並得出「採用這個方法的家長們也會很快就會對於小孩日趨嚴重的視力不良和學校成績不佳的問題感到如釋重負。」

Step 3 最後，簡短地總結。

 整合能力強化 ❹ 參考範文 ▶ *MP3 009* 

經由先前的演練後，現在請看整篇範文並聆聽音檔

Aside from the fact that prolonged viewing on the smartphone does cause eyestrain and headaches, smartphones do make children more distracted in their academic study. The statement would make today's parents increasingly worrisome, since their kids all have been interacting with digital technologies. This has greatly influenced children's ways of learning, as they rely heavily on short videos and shorter E-contents that are easily grasped. Navigation on longer texts, which are required during kids' academic studies in both high schools and colleges, may seem unlikely. This can result in a poor performance in reading, and a lack of enough vocabularies to express ourselves clearly.

除了長期觀看智慧型手機會造成眼睛疲勞和頭痛之外，智慧型手機確實會讓小孩在學術研讀中更為分心。這項陳述讓今日的家長們憂心忡忡，因為他們的孩子一直都與數位科技有所互動。隨著他們很大程度地仰賴訊息容易吸收的短視頻和較為簡短的電子內容，這大幅地影響了孩子們的學習方式。在高中和大學求學期間，必需具備能瀏覽較長的文字內容，對他們來說似乎是鑽火得冰。這會導致閱讀表現不佳，以及缺乏足夠的字彙以清楚表達自我。

Studies have found that families who customarily sit in a study room reading, even for just an hour a day, have a significant boost to children's learning. Not using the phone is probably the key, and for the great habit to take hold is perhaps another contributor. Children are bound to take the good habit with them throughout their lives, thus, having a tremendous influence on their later lives.

研究發現，具有在讀書間坐下閱讀習慣的家庭，即使僅僅只有花費每天一小時的時間，對於小孩的學習有顯著的提升。不使用手機可能就是關鍵所在，而要讓這個絕佳的習慣成形或許是另一個促成的因素。孩童必定會在終其一生都帶著這樣的好習慣，因此，對於他們之後的生活也會有極大的影響。

Good habit formation seems to be the cure for today's parents, who have no idea how to teach their kids. Making kids understood that a few hours away from the smartphones will actually do them good. Reading together in a study room is just an example. A few hours of outdoor activities or playing music instrument can also work. Parents adopting this method will soon find themselves relieved of kid's increasingly poor eyesight and bad school report cards.

養成好習慣似乎是現今父母們在不知道要如何教育子女時的解方。讓孩子們了解到遠離智慧型手機幾個小時對他們來說實際上是有益的。在讀書間一起讀書只是一個舉例。幾個小時的戶外活動或是演奏音樂樂器也能奏效。採用這個方法的家長們也會很快就會對於小孩日趨嚴重的視力不良和學校成績不佳的問題感到如釋重負。

To sum up, habit formation is the key, and engaging in other outdoor activities or reading a few hours a day consistently for a few years will be conducive to children's health and school performance.

總之，習慣的養成就是關鍵，從事其他的戶外活動或者是每日閱讀幾小時幾年下來持之以恆都對於小孩的健康和學校表現有所助益。

UNIT 03

在鎂光燈背後，運動員確實付出許多不為人知的努力。他們都受到良好的訓練，而如果扣除掉天賦這點，有哪些因素是讓他們勝出的關鍵呢？

Writing Task 2

TOPIC

We have been misled into believing that those elite athletes do not necessarily have to work industriously. They are naturally born that way, but that is so not true. They all have received excellent trainings. In addition to their innate talents, what are other factors that you deem might help them outshine other athletes. Use specific reasons and examples to back up your standpoints.

Write at least 250 words

整合能力強化 ❶ 實際演練

請搭配左頁的題目和並構思和完成大作文的演練。

整合能力強化 ❷ 單句中譯英演練

❶ 運動員都具有完美個肌肉組織，而且毫秒之差就會決定最終的贏家。

【參考答案】

Athletes all have perfect musculature, and differences in milliseconds will determine the ultimate winner.

❷ 不論是在電視上或是在巨大的體育館中，我們大多數的人都曾看過一些菁英運動員。

【參考答案】

Most of us have seen some of elite athletes, whether it is on TV or at the tremendous stadium.

❸ 獨特的燈光打在他們完美的體態上讓我們都忘卻了他們訓練所付出的苦工。

【參考答案】

The glamorous light hitting on their perfect body makes us forget the hard work of their training.

❹ 他們都經歷嚴格的訓練並且有很棒的教練，不過在日常生活中，我們鮮少將像是慣例、習慣和管理風險列入加以思考，而這也是鑑別優劣的原因。

____

____

【參考答案】

They all have undergone rigorous trainings and have a great coach, yet in daily life we rarely give factors, such as routine, habits, handling risks a second thought, and that is the reason that separates the wheat from the chaff.

❺ 儘管運動員的天賦可能有所影響，導致一個人的學習能夠易如反掌，而其他人卻是差強人意。

____

____

【參考答案】

Although athletes' innateness may play a role, resulting in one's learning so readily, while others scarcely learn them at all.

❻ 在《為什麼我們這樣生活，那樣工作？》，從費爾普斯的例子當中，書籍提供了如何能鶴立雞群的解釋。

【參考答案】
In *The Power of Habit: why we do what we do and how to change*, it shed lights on how to stand out from the crowd, as can be seen in Phelps' case.

❼ 在深夜的密西根湖中游泳就幫助了費爾普斯維持了他表現水平的恆定性，即使護目鏡脫落。

【參考答案】
Swimming in a Michigan pool in the dark will help Phelps maintain the constancy of the level of his performance, even if there is a goggle failure.

❽ 實際上，這是個關鍵，因為沒有人可以有第二次的表現機會，而且沒有所謂的「下一次」。

【參考答案】
This is actually the key because no one cannot redo the performance and there is no more the so called "the next time".

❾ 替任何意料之外的事情作足準備比起訓練時的強度和運動員體內的肌肉數量多寡等等的都更為重要。此外，在夜晚的湖中游泳需要的是勇氣和能夠面對未知的能力。

【參考答案】

To be ready for any surprise is more important than intensity of the training and the number of muscles in an athlete's body, and so on. Moreover, swimming in the dark lake requires one's courage and one's ability to handle the unknown.

❿ 而且，習慣和慣例的運動排程對於一個運動員能夠處於狀態良好的情況和準備就緒參賽扮演了重要的角色。

【參考答案】

Also, habits and routine schedules also play a vital role for an athlete to be in the good condition and ready for the contest.

TOPIC

We have been misled into believing that those elite athletes do not necessarily have to work industriously. They are naturally born that way, but that is so not true. They all have received excellent trainings. In addition to their innate talents, what are other factors that you deem might help them outshine other athletes. Use specific reasons and examples to back up your standpoints.

搭配的暢銷書

- The Power of Habit: why we do what we do and how to change《為什麼我們這樣生活，那樣工作？》

Step 1

- 先定義「運動員都具有完美的肌肉組織，而且毫秒之差就會決定最終的贏家。」
- 然後反思，如果是這樣子的話，要贏得比賽，哪個因素實際上會扮演更重要的角色呢？

Step 2

- **接著鋪陳**，「不論是在電視上或是在巨型的體育館中，我們大多數的人都曾看過一些菁英運動員。獨特的燈光打在他們完美的體態上讓我們都忘卻了他們訓練所付出的苦工。
- **最後導入主題**，不過在日常生活中，我們鮮少將像是慣例、習慣和管理風險列入加以思考，而這也是鑑別優劣的原因。

Step 3

- **敘述**，並排除掉天賦影響運動員表現。

Step 4

- **搭配暢銷書舉例**，並指出「要充分準備且能面對未知是關鍵所在」。
- **得出另一個結論**，深夜的密西根湖中游泳訓練和維持表現穩定性，「進一步得出替任何意料之外的事情作足準備比起訓練時的強度和運動員體內的肌肉數量多寡等等的都更為重要。」
- **最後強化論點**，習慣和慣例的運動排程對於一個運動員能夠處於狀態良好的情況和準備就緒參賽扮演了重要的角色。

Step 5

- 最後簡短地總結。

 整合能力強化 ❹ 參考範文 ▶ *MP3 010* 

經由先前的演練後，現在請看整篇範文並聆聽音檔

Athletes all have perfect musculature, and differences in milliseconds will determine the ultimate winner. If so, which factors will actually be relatively or comparatively important, when it comes to winning.

運動員都具有完美的肌肉組織，而且毫秒之差就會決定最終的贏家。如果是這樣子的話，當提到獲勝，哪個因素實際上會較為或相對來說更為重要呢？

Most of us have seen some of elite athletes, whether it is on TV or at the tremendous stadium. The glamorous light hitting on their perfect body makes us forget the hard work of their training. They all have undergone rigorous trainings and have a great coach, **yet in daily life we rarely give factors, such as routine, habits, handling risks a second thought**, and that is the reason that separates the wheat from the chaff.

不論是在電視上或是在巨型的體育館中，我們大多數的人都曾看過一些菁英運動員。獨特的燈光打在他們完美的體態上讓我們都忘卻了他們訓練所付出的苦工。他們都經歷嚴格的訓練並且有很棒的教練，不過在日常生活中，我們鮮少將像是慣例、習慣和管理風險列入加以思考，而這也是鑑別優劣的原因。

Although athletes' innateness may play a role, resulting in one's learning so readily, while others scarcely learn them at all. If we are looking at hand-picked Olympian athletes, we have to disregard inborn traits.

儘管運動員的天賦可能有所影響，導致一個人的學習能夠易如反掌，而其他人卻是差強人意。如果我們是以奧林匹亞的選手為標準的話，我們要忽略掉與生俱來的特質。

In *The Power of Habit: why we do what we do and how to change*, it shed lights on how to stand out from the crowd, as can be seen in Phelps' case. To be fully prepared and to face the uncertainty are the key. Swimming in a Michigan pool in the dark will help Phelps maintain the constancy of the level of his performance, even if there is a goggle failure. This is actually the key because no one cannot redo the performance and there is no more the so called “the next time”. To be ready for any surprise is more important than intensity in the training and the number of muscles in an athlete’s body, and so on. Moreover, swimming in the dark lake requires one’s courage and one’s ability to handle the unknown. Also, habits and routine schedules also play a vital role for an athlete to be in the good condition and ready for the contest.

在《為什麼我們這樣生活，那樣工作？》，從費爾普斯的例子當中，書籍提供了如何能鶴立雞群的解釋。要充分準備且能面對未知是關鍵所在。在深夜的密西根湖中游泳就幫助了費爾普斯維持了他表現水平的恆定性，即使護目鏡脫落。實際上，這是個關鍵，因為沒有人可以有第二次的表現機會，而且沒有所謂的「下一次」。替任何意料之外的事情作足準備比起訓練時的強度和運動員體內的肌肉數量多寡等等的都更為重要。此外，在夜晚的湖中游泳需要的是勇氣和能夠面對未知的能力。而且，習慣和慣例的運動排程對於一個運動員能夠處於狀態良好的情況和準備就緒參賽扮演了重要的角色。

To sum up, a combination of habits, routine, and handling risks is the key for an athlete to outperform other opponents.

總之，一位運動員要能勝過其他競爭對手，習慣、慣例和管理風險是關鍵所在。

UNIT 04

儘管現在人普遍仰賴傳統醫療，但是有些疾病無法僅單純靠服藥或採用傳統醫療就能治癒，這也是為什麼其他人在替代醫療領域尋求解方。當中又有那些症狀可能無法單靠傳統醫療治療呢？替代醫療的優點又有哪些？

Writing Task 2

TOPIC

In today's world, we are heavily reliant on traditional medicine. However, there are still some diseases that cannot be removed simply by taking traditional medicine. Others are trying to seek for the advice in the field of alternative medicine. What is the advantage of using alternative medicine? Describe some symptoms that cannot be fully cured by traditional medicine.

Write at least 250 words

整合能力強化 ❶ 實際演練

請搭配左頁的題目和並構思和完成大作文的演練。

整合能力強化 ❷ 單句中譯英演練

❶ 在診療所，有嚴重疾病的病患會顯示出豐富的情緒反應。較仔細地檢視後能揭露出痛苦的程度。

____

____

【參考答案】

In the dispensary, patients with severe illnesses will exhibit a whole gamut of emotional responses. A closer inspection can reveal how painful that is.

❷ 這些症狀是嚴峻的，且無法僅單純靠服藥或採用傳統醫療就能治癒。

____

____

【參考答案】

These symptoms are austere, and cannot be cured simply by taking medicine or adopting traditional medicine.

❸ 根據其中一本暢銷書，《每一天都是全新的時刻：用創造預想畫面探索內在的自己，得到生命中所真心渴望的》，作者列出了幾個導致一個人患有一些生病或情緒上的疾病的範例，而有些疾病的根源是來自於我們的創傷。

____

____

【參考答案】

According to one of the bestsellers, *Creative Visualization: Use the Power of Your Imagination to Create What You Want in Your Life*, the author has listed several examples that lead to one to come down with some diseases or emotional illness, and some root causes of the diseases come from our trauma.

❹ 在其中的一個描述中，癌症是由無法根除的累積壓力所引起的。一個人的情緒沒有釋放的出口。

____

____

【參考答案】

In one of the depictions, cancer is caused by accumulated pressure that cannot be resolved. One's emotions do not have an outlet.

❺ 壓抑的感受會導致無法解決的衝突。一個人要活得健康，就必須要釋放那些情緒。

____

____

【參考答案】

The suppressed feelings will result in a clash that cannot be solved. For a person to be live well, one must release those emotions.

❻ 大多數的時候，隱藏在那些情緒的背後是複雜的因素。我們必須要迎面面對問題，才能在情感、心理和精神層面上都健康。

____

____

【參考答案】

Most of the time, what is behind those emotions is complicated factors. We have to face the problem head-on to be emotionally, psychologically, and psychiatrically healthy.

❼ 作者也提到採用視覺化的圖像當作能夠有效治療疾病的方式，而且俗話說「預防是勝於治療的。」

____

____

【參考答案】

The author also mentions adopting visualized pictures as a way to effectively cure the disease, and as a saying goes "prevention is better than cure".

❽ 有些人利用旅行、走入林地和觀賞海洋美景以暫時忘卻問題的存在，但是當他們結束度假後，問題仍在那裡。

____

____

【參考答案】
Some people use traveling, going into the woods, and viewing beautiful ocean scenery as the way to forgetting the existence of the problem for a while, but when they are back from the vacation, the problem is still there.

9 一個人的工作壓力、在工作中遇到的不滿意或是孩童時期的創傷仍舊會佔據一個人的心理。偶爾，有些思想和不好的記憶會在你走路到公司的途中或是當你在等一位朋友一起喝杯咖啡時又浮現出腦海。

【參考答案】
One's work pressure, dissatisfaction at work or childhood trauma is still occupied in one's mind. Every now and then, some thoughts and bad memories will appear on your walk to the office or when you are waiting for a friend for a coffee.

10 這也就是我們為什麼需要替代性醫療來協助我們，逐步地移除那些抑制我們的情緒。

【參考答案】
That is why we do need alternative medicine to assist us to gradually remove those emotions that inhibit us.

TOPIC

In today's world, we are heavily reliant on traditional medicine. However, there are still some diseases that cannot be removed simply by taking traditional medicine. Others are trying to seek for the advice in the field of alternative medicine. What is the advantage of using alternative medicine? Describe some symptoms that cannot be fully cured by traditional medicine.

搭配的暢銷書

■ Creative Visualization: Use the Power of Your Imagination to Create What You Want in Your Life《每一天都是全新的時刻：用創造預想畫面探索內在的自己，得到生命中所真心渴望的》

Step 1 ■ 用在診療中的實況破題並引入主題，並指出「病人無法僅單純靠服藥或採用傳統醫療就能治癒」。

■ 接著以暢銷書論點描述，「有些疾病的根源是來自於我們的創傷。在其中的一個描述中，癌症是由無法根除的累積壓力所引起的。」

■ 提到釋放情緒的重要性。

■ 提到採用視覺化的圖像當作能夠有效治療疾病的方式，而且俗話說「預防是勝於治療的。」

Step 2 ■ 提到以其他的休閒方式進行排解問題，但問題依舊存在。

■ 最後指出，「這也就是我們為什麼需要替代性醫療來協助我們，逐步地移除那些抑制我們的情緒。你確實必須要經歷一些過程，實際上去原諒一個特定的事件或一個人，然後，在那之後，你才能獲得情感上的健康。」

Step 3 ■ 簡短地總結。

整合能力強化 ❹ 參考範文 ▶ *MP3 011*

經由先前的演練後，現在請看整篇範文並聆聽音檔

In the dispensary, patients with severe illnesses will exhibit a whole gamut of emotional responses. A closer inspection can reveal how painful that is. These symptoms are austere, and cannot be cured simply by taking medicine or adopting traditional medicine. According to one of the bestsellers, *Creative Visualization: Use the Power of Your Imagination to Create What You Want in Your Life*, the author has listed several examples that lead to one to come down with some diseases or emotional illness, and some root causes of the diseases come from our trauma.

在診療所，有嚴重疾病的病患會顯示出豐富的情緒反應。較仔細地檢視後能揭露出痛苦的程度。這些症狀是嚴峻的，且無法僅單純靠服藥或採用傳統醫療就能治癒。根據其中一本暢銷書，《每一天都是全新的時刻：用創造預想畫面探索內在的自己，得到生命中所真心渴望的》，作者列出了幾個導致一個人患有一些生病或情緒上的疾病的範例，而有些疾病的根源是來自於我們的創傷。

In one of the depictions, cancer is caused by accumulated pressure that cannot be resolved. One's emotions do not have an outlet. The suppressed feelings will result in a clash that cannot be solved. For a person to be live well, one must release those emotions. Most of the time, what is behind those emotions is complicated factors. We have to face the problem head-on to emotionally, psychologically, and psychiatrically healthy. The author also mentions adopting visualized pictures as a way to effectively cure the disease, and as a saying goes "prevention is better than cure".

在其中的一個描述中，癌症是由無法根除的累積壓力所引起的。一個人的情緒沒有釋放的出口。壓抑的感受會導致無法解決的衝突。一個人要活得健康，就必須要釋放那些情緒。大多數的時候，隱藏在那些情緒的背後是複雜的因素。我們必須要迎面面對問題，才能在情感、心理和精神層面上都健康。作者也提到採用視覺化的圖像當作能夠有效治療疾病的方式，而且俗話說「預防是勝於治療的。」

Some people use traveling, going into the woods, and viewing beautiful ocean scenery as the way to forgetting the existence of the problem for a while, but when they are back from the vacation, the problem is still there. One's work pressure, dissatisfaction at work or childhood trauma is still occupied in one's mind. Every now and then, some thoughts and bad memories will appear on your walk to the office or when you are waiting for a friend for a coffee. That is why we do need alternative medicine to assist us to gradually remove those emotions that inhibit us. You will certainly have to experience some phases to actually forgive a certain event or a person, and after that you will be emotionally healthy.

有些人利用旅行、走入林地和觀賞海洋美景以暫時忘卻問題的存在，但是當他們結束度假後，問題仍在那裡。一個人的工作壓力、在工作中遇到的不滿意或是孩童時期的創傷仍舊會佔據一個人的心理。偶爾，有些思想和不好的記憶會在你走路到公司的途中或是當你在等一位朋友一起喝杯咖啡時又浮現出腦海。這也就是我們為什麼需要替代性醫療來協助我們，逐步地移除那些抑制我們的情緒。你確實必須要經歷一些過程，實際上去原諒一個特定的事件或一個人，然後，在那之後，你才能獲得情感上的健康。

To sum up, I think alternative medicine does have its advantages when it comes to one's health, and cannot be replaced by traditional medicine.

總之，當提到一個人的健康時，我認為替代醫療確實有它的優點，且無法被傳統醫療取代。

UNIT 05

每個人對於理想和想像中的居住環境各異，有些人甚至已經達成目標，搬到理想的湖邊小屋居住了。對你來說，想像中的居住環境又必須要具備有哪些條件呢？

Writing Task 2

TOPIC

Some envision living near the ocean when they are about to retire. Others have already purchased a lake house and fully enjoy the view there. Still others are trying to picture their ideal, imaginary living place so that they can stay away from horrific traffic jams and crowds. What is you imaginary living place. Describe the living place in details.

Write at least 250 words

整合能力強化 ❶ 實際演練

請搭配左頁的題目和並構思和完成大作文的演練。

整合能力強化 ❷ 單句中譯英演練

❶ 我的想像中的居住環境必須要是在靠近北方，如此我才能目睹可愛的雌性棕熊攜帶幼熊的景象。

____

____

【參考答案】

My imaginary living place has to be set near the north where I can witness the view of adorable female brown bears with their cubs.

❷ 房子後院必須要裝置著一打的腐朽樹木，這樣一來蜜蜂就能在那裡找到庇護所。

____

____

【參考答案】

The backyard of the house must be furnished with a dozen decayed trees so that honeybees will find their shelters in there.

❸ 每隔幾個月，我能享用蜜蜂的生產成果，然後讚譽自然的驚奇。我會耕種千變萬化的花來報償牠們的辛苦以作為互換。

____

____

【參考答案】

Every few months, I can enjoy honeybees' production, and praise the natural wonder. In exchange, I will cultivate kaleidoscopic flowers to reward their hard work.

❹ 我的家庭成員能目睹不同類型的花所創造出童話故事般的景象。

【參考答案】

Different types of flowers will create a fairy-tale like view for my family members.

❺ 那些花朵和不同類型的植物會形成一個小型的生態系統，你能在大樹葉或已盛開的花朵下方找到獨特的昆蟲。

【參考答案】

Those flowers and various types of plants will form a small ecosystem, where one can find peculiar insects hiding under large leaves or blossomed flowers.

❻ 在前院，會有可耕種的土地，能用於種植不同的莓果和蔬菜。

【參考答案】

In the front yard, there will be arable lands for the cultivation of different berries and vegetables.

❼ 每當有拜訪者來的時候，我的確可以邀請他們到房裡，並侍奉上親手摘採的莓果給他們。他們會感到體力盡復，然後有心情去參觀一下我們的地下室。

____

____

【參考答案】

Whenever there are visitors, I can actually invite them in the house and serve the hand-picked berries for them. They will feel recharged and have the mood to take a look at our basement.

❽ 在地下室，我會試著仿效不同菌種能夠生長的人工環境，如此一來我的家庭成員每天就能享用新鮮健康的湯。

____

____

【參考答案】

In the basement, I will try to mimic an artificial setting for various mushrooms to grow so that my family members can have a fresh, healthy soup every day.

❾ 在客廳，則會有一個大型的火爐，這樣大家就會感到溫暖。

【參考答案】
In our living room, there is going to be a large stove so that people can feel warm.

❿ 當然，火爐會放置在客廳中間，這樣大家能夠聚在一塊並享用烤肉。火爐會非常大個，這樣放置兩頭山羊都綽綽有餘。

【參考答案】
Of course, it is going to be set in the middle of the living room where people can gather and have a barbecue. It will be immensely large so that putting two goats will surely enough.

整合能力強化 ❸ 段落拓展

TOPIC

Some envision living near the ocean when they are about to retire. Others have already purchased a lake house and fully enjoy the view there. Still others are trying to picture their ideal, imaginary living place so that they can stay away from horrific traffic jams and crowds. What is you imaginary living place. Describe the living place in details.

Step 1

- 首段第一句直接破題，直接表明「我的想像中的居住環境必須要是在靠近北方，如此我才能目睹可愛的雌性棕熊攜帶幼熊的景象。」，表達出大概的位置和欲看到的景象。
- 接著描述出後院想要打造成的環境，並生動化這些描述，當中包含朽木、蜜蜂和小型生態系統等等。

Step 2

- 次段描述前院，「在前院，會有可耕種的土地，能用於種植不同的莓果和蔬菜。」，並接續引出下一個段落，也就是地下室。

Step 3 ■ 次一段接續描述地下室，「在地下室，我會試著仿效不同菌種能夠生長的人工環境，如此一來我的家庭成員每天就能享用新鮮健康的湯。」，並穿插和接續描述客廳（因為範文字數所限，加上是限定在考場要寫完這篇內容，所以合併在一段）。

Step 4 最後簡單地總結。

整合能力強化 ❹ 參考範文 ▶ *MP3 012*

經由先前的演練後，現在請看整篇範文並聆聽音檔

My imaginary living place has to be set near the north where I can witness the view of adorable female brown bears with their cubs. The backyard of the house must be furnished with a dozen decayed trees so that honeybees will find their shelters in there.

我的想像中的居住環境必須要是在靠近北方，如此我才能目睹可愛的雌性棕熊攜帶幼熊的景象。房子後院必須要裝置著一打的腐朽樹木，這樣一來蜜蜂就能在那裡找到庇護所。

Every few months, I can enjoy honeybees' production, and praise the natural wonder. In exchange, I will cultivate kaleidoscopic flowers to reward their hard work. Different types of flowers will create a fairy-tale like view for my family members. Those flowers and various types of plants will form a small ecosystem, where one can find peculiar insects hiding under large leaves or blossomed flowers.

每隔幾個月，我能享用蜜蜂的生產成果，然後讚譽自然的驚奇。我會耕種千變萬化的花來報償牠們的辛苦以作為互換。我的家庭成員能目睹不同類型的花所創造出童話故事般的景象。那些花朵和不同類型的植物會形成一個小型的生態系統，你能在大片樹葉或已盛開的花朵下方找到獨特的昆蟲。

In the front yard, there will be arable lands for the cultivation of different berries and vegetables. Whenever there are visitors, I can actually invite them in the house and serve the hand-picked berries for them. They will feel recharged and have the mood to take a look at our basement.

在前院，會有可耕種的土地，能用於種植不同的莓果和蔬菜。每當有拜訪者來的時候，我的確可以邀請他們到房裡，並侍奉上親手摘採的莓果給他們。他們會感到體力盡復，然後有心情去參觀一下我們的地下室。

In the basement, I will try to mimic an artificial setting for various mushrooms to grow so that my family members can have a fresh, healthy soup every day. In our living room, there is going to be a large stove so that people can feel warm. Of course, it is going to be set in the middle of the living room where people can gather and have a barbecue. It will be immensely large so that putting two goats will surely enough. This will certainly create a perfect place for the retirement and students' summer camp.

在地下室，我會試著仿效不同菌種能夠生長的人工環境，如此一來我的家庭成員每天就能享用新鮮健康的湯。在客廳，則會有一個大型的火爐，這樣大家就會感到溫暖。當然，火爐會放置在客廳中間，這樣大家能夠聚在一塊並享用烤肉。火爐會非常大個，這樣放置兩頭山羊都綽綽有餘。這樣確實會創造一個適合退休和學生夏季露營的完美場地。

To sum up, this is the imaginary living place pleasing to look at and wonderfully to live in.

總之，這是個賞心悅目且絕佳的想像中的居住環境。

UNIT 06

幾乎每間公司都經歷過這個階段，雖有幾項品質良好的產品，但卻似乎乏人問津，如何抓住顧客眼球就顯得特別重要了。你對廣告的看法又是如何呢？你認為廣告一定要牽涉到任何花費嗎？鶴立雞群的關鍵是什麼呢？

Writing Task 2

TOPIC

There is no denying that to catch the eyeballs from customers you have to do some serious work. To make immense profits is not as easy as it seems.

Some companies hire people who are great at storytelling techniques, whereas others try to think outside of the box. What are your viewpoints on advertising? Does advertising have to be involved in spending a great deal of money? What is the key to stand out? Use specific examples.

Write at least 250 words

整合能力強化 ❶ 實際演練

請搭配左頁的題目和並構思和完成大作文的演練。

整合能力強化 ❷ 單句中譯英演練 ▶ *MP3 009*

❶ 有些人鋪陳劇情的方式，如同在製作精品工藝，這樣一來廣告的商品對消費者來說就具有說服力，而其他人利用的技巧就很笨拙以至於收到了顧客們連連回絕。

____

____

【參考答案】

Some people make a craft of braiding the storylines so that advertised products can be convincing to customers, while others use the skills so clumsy that get repeated rejections from the customers.

❷ 顯然，在今日的競爭世界，創新、創意和說故事技巧都是重中之重，如果公司想要獲取鉅額的獲利的話。

____

____

【參考答案】

Apparently, in today's competitive world, innovation, creativity, and storytelling skills are exceedingly important, if the company wants to make tremendous profits.

❸ 要如何出類拔萃是主要的考量，而問題依舊存在：要如何行動呢？在《第一份工作》，農場奇才能充當為今日主題的範例，並且向我們顯示出該如何突破和創新以抓住顧客的眼球。

【參考答案】
How to stand out from the crowd is the central concern, and the question remains: how. In *First Jobs*, the farm prodigy can serve as an example to today's topic and shows us how to breakthrough and innovate to catch the eyeballs of the customers.

❹ 其中之一可能的方式是品牌創建，但是在農場奇才的例子中，是關於在停滯的階段中尋求突破。

【參考答案】
Branding is perhaps one of the ways, but in the farm prodigy's case, it is about the breakthrough through the stagnant stage.

❺ 幾乎每間公司都經歷過這個階段，因而有幾項品質良好的產品，但卻似乎乏人問津。

【參考答案】
Almost every company has experienced the stage that it has several products with good quality but no one seems to pay attention to them.

❻ 在故事中，「這些黃瓜賣相佳，但卻因為已經放在陰涼處過久，而無法運送。」如何使用廣告和行銷的力量讓這些產品獲得關注並且最終銷售成功是關鍵所在。

【參考答案】
In the story, "These cucumbers were in good shape but they could not be shipped because they had been in the cooler for long." How to use the power of advertising and marketing to make these products getting attention and eventually be purchased is the key.

❼ 這位男孩的父親在男孩身旁放置兩個手寫的廣告招牌，上面寫著「羅伯特在此」。

【參考答案】
The boy's father put two written signs next to the boy, writing "Robert Is Here."

❽ 「誰是羅伯特」已經引起人們的關注，因此，讓男孩家裡也有了穩定的收入。

【參考答案】
"Who is Robert" has garnered people's attention, therefore, making a steady income for the boy's family.

❾ 要讓廣告發揮效果，你確實必須要嘗試一些「自成一格」的方式以獲取足夠的關注。

____

____

【參考答案】
For the advertising to work, you do have to try something unorthodox to get enough attention.

❿ 這個男孩不需要懂電腦，但是廣告招牌卻已經成了觀光景點。當人們實際上在使用電腦時，你就知道了確切的地點所在。

____

____

【參考答案】
The boy doesn't have to know the computer, but the sign has become the tourist spot. When people actually use the computer, you know the exact location.

整合能力強化 ❸ 段落拓展

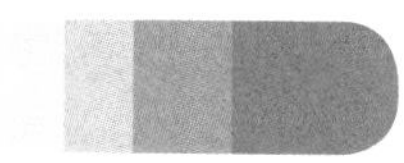

TOPIC

There is no denying that to catch the eyeballs from customers you have to do some serious work. To make immense profits is not as easy as it seems.

Some companies hire people who are great at storytelling techniques, whereas others try to think outside of the box. What are your viewpoints on advertising? Does advertising have to be involved in spending a great deal of money? What is the key to stand out? Use specific examples.

搭配的暢銷書

■ First Jobs《第一份工作》

Step 1

■ 以更好的譬喻和鋪陳方式切入主題，「有些人鋪陳劇情的方式，如同在製作精品工藝，這樣一來廣告的商品對消費者來說就具有說服力，而其他人利用的技巧就很笨拙以至於收到了顧客們連連回絕。」

■ 最後說明，顯然，在今日的競爭世界，創新、創意和說故事技巧都是重中之重，如果公司想要獲取鉅額的獲利的話。

Step 2

■ 搭配暢銷書講述要如何才能出類拔萃。

■ 講述其中的方法，其中之一可能的方式是品牌創建。

■ 講述要突破的困境，品質良好，但卻似乎乏人問津的產品，要如何突破。

Step 3

■ 講述故事中的困境，「這些黃瓜賣相佳，但卻因為已經放在陰涼處過久，而無法運送。」

■ 進一步指出，如何使用廣告和行銷的力量讓這些產品獲得關注並且最終銷售成功是關鍵所在。

■ 男孩父親運用其他方式讓他們「自成一格」，以獲取足夠的關注，他們甚至不需要懂科技產品。

Step 4 最後簡單地總結，發展出個人特色並抓住顧客眼球。

整合能力強化 ❹ 參考範文 ▶ *MP3 013*

經由先前的演練後，現在請看整篇範文並聆聽音檔

Some people make a craft of braiding the storylines so that advertised products can be convincing to customers, while others use the skills so clumsy that get repeated rejections from the customers. Apparently, in today's competitive world, innovation, creativity, and storytelling skills are exceedingly important, if the company wants to make tremendous profits.

有些人鋪陳劇情的方式，如同在製作精品工藝，這樣一來廣告的商品對消費者來說就具有說服力，而其他人利用的技巧就很笨拙以至於收到了顧客們連連回絕。顯然，在今日的競爭世界，創新、創意和說故事技巧都是重中之重，如果公司想要獲取鉅額的獲利的話。

How to stand out from the crowd is the central concern, and the question remains: how. In *First Jobs*, the farm prodigy can serve as an example to today's topic and shows us how to breakthrough and innovate to catch the eyeballs of the customers. Branding is perhaps one of the ways, but in the farm prodigy's case, it is about the breakthrough through the stagnant stage. Almost every company has experienced the stage that it has several products with good quality but no one seems to pay attention to them.

要如何出類拔萃是主要的考量，而問題依舊存在：要如何行動呢？在《第一份工作》，農場奇才能充當為今日主題的範例，並且向我們顯示出該如何突破和創新以抓住顧客的眼球。其中之一可能的方式是品牌創建，但是在農場奇才的例子中，是關於在停滯的階段中尋求突破。幾乎每間公司都經歷過這個階段，因而有幾項品質良好的產品，但卻似乎乏人問津。

In the story, **"These cucumbers were in good shape but they could not be shipped because they had been in the cooler for long."** How to use the power of advertising and marketing to make these products getting attention and eventually be purchased is the key. The boy's father put two written signs next to the boy, writing "Robert Is Here." "Who is Robert" has garnered people's attention, therefore, making a steady income for the boy's family. For the advertising to work, you do have to try something unorthodox to get enough attention. The boy doesn't have to know the computer, but the sign has become the tourist spot. When people actually use the computer, you know the exact location.

在故事中，「這些黃瓜賣相佳，但卻因為已經放在陰涼處過久，而無法運送。」如何使用廣告和行銷的力量讓這些產品獲得關注並且最終銷售成功是關鍵所在。這位男孩的父親在男孩身旁放置兩個手寫的廣告招牌，上面寫著「羅伯特在此」。「誰是羅伯特」已經引起人們的關注，因此，讓男孩家裡也有了穩定的收入。要讓廣告發揮效果，你確實必須要嘗試一些「自成一格」的方式以獲取足夠的關注。這個男孩不需要懂電腦，但是廣告招牌卻已經成了觀光景點。當人們實際上在使用電腦時，你就知道了確切的地點所在。

To sum up, trying something unorthodox and creative is the key. When you know the trick of getting customer's eyeballs, your corporate ladder towards the CEO of advertising gets closer or you will learn how to make money.

總之，嘗試一些「自成一家」且具創意的方式是關鍵所在。當你懂了抓住顧客眼球的訣竅，你朝向廣告執行長的工作之路就更近一步了，或是你就學會了如何賺錢了。

UNIT 07

儘管政府和健康專家們的努力和勸說，新品牌的手搖飲料店如雨後春筍般不斷地浮現在已經飽和的市場裡。消費者更是人手一杯，促成這個現象有許多原因，而你覺得在未來，手搖飲這樣的飲料會大幅減少嗎？

Writing Task 2

TOPIC

Despite efforts made by governments and health specialists, unhealthy drinks still exist. Ingredients in those drinks and manipulation from companies all make this phenomenon hard to tackle. People just cannot stand the magic from those drinks. Do you think that in the near future, hand-shaken drinks will be greatly reduced? Use specific examples to elucidate the phenomenon.

Write at least 250 words

整合能力強化 ❶ 實際演練

請搭配左頁的題目和並構思和完成大作文的演練。

整合能力強化 ❷ 單句中譯英演練 ▶ *MP3 009*

❶ 新品牌的手搖飲料店如雨後春筍般不斷地浮現在已經飽和的市場裡，但是手搖飲料店家們在某些程度上懂得要如何操控消費者。

____

____

【參考答案】

New brands of the tea shake outlets are constantly popping up in the already saturated markets, but they somehow understand how to manipulate buyers.

❷ 在 Instagram 上上傳過時飲品的照片的話，人們會想到你是住在哪個星球上。

____

____

【參考答案】

Uploading the picture of the old-fashioned drinks on the Instagram, people think what planet do you live on.

❸ 飲料公司完全意識到這個現象，特別是在現今的社會裡。通常，人都會隨身攜帶智慧型手機，且手機上會安裝好 Instagram。

____

____

【參考答案】

Beverage companies are fully aware of this phenomenon, especially in today's society. Normally, people carry a smartphone with them, and most with the Instagram installed.

❹ 每當他們有閒暇時間的時候，就會偶爾檢視下新訊息。儘管有些創意風味的飲料並未讓顧客欲罷不能，這樣的操控卻出奇地奏效。

____

____

【參考答案】

They check new messages every now and then whenever they have the time. The manipulation works exceedingly well, although some creative flavors of the drink do not make customers glued to the store.

❺ 不論這些飲料是否真的美味出奇，我們的健康都受到這些手搖飲大幅地影響了，導致我們重新思考著每日所攝取的糖分。

____

____

【參考答案】

Whether these drinks are genuinely scrumptious, our health has been greatly influenced by those hand-shaken drinks, leading us to rethink about the consumption of sugar in a day.

❻ 因為青少年和年輕人是主要的購買族群，健康專家們對於現今糖尿病在這些族群中更為普遍的趨勢感到擔憂。

【參考答案】

Health experts are worried that diabetes is bound to be more prevalent among today's teenagers and young people since they are the main purchasers.

❼ 醫生和大學教授都警告父母攝取過多的糖分的嚴重性，因為孩童的認知發展可能會因此而惡化。

【參考答案】

Doctors and college professors are warning parents of the grisliness of consuming too much sugar because children's cognitive development may be worsened.

❽ 不分年齡，人們會有購買飲料的習慣。在下課或午餐期間，你沒有購買飲料的話，你會有奇怪的感覺。

【參考答案】

Regardless of age, people will form the habit of purchasing the drink. When you are not having the drink during the lunch time at work or after school, you feel an odd sense of eccentricity.

❾ 你的腦部會傳遞訊息給你，讓你覺得必須要購買飲料以覺得滿足，儘管有些人購買飲料只是要迎合 Instagram 的追蹤者。

____

____

【參考答案】

Your brain signals a message that you have to buy a drink to feel satisfied, although some just want a drink to please Instagram followers.

❿ 當手搖飲已經跟智慧型手機的使用有關聯時，就成了更為複雜的問題了。儘管健康專家和行為科學家兩者所做的努力，人們仍舊會出於新奇感而做出購買行為。

____

____

【參考答案】

When the hand-shaken drinks have been linked with the use of smartphone, it has become an even more complicated problem. Despite the effort made by both Health experts and behavior scientists, still people are making the purchase out of a novelty.

TOPIC

Despite efforts made by governments and health specialists, unhealthy drinks still exist. Ingredients in those drinks and manipulation from companies all make this phenomenon hard to tackle. People just cannot stand the magic from those drinks. Do you think that in the near future, hand-shaken drinks will be greatly reduced? Use specific examples to elucidate the phenomenon.

Step 1

- **先鋪陳並豐富化切入句**，「新品牌的手搖飲料店如雨後春筍般不斷地浮現在已經飽和的市場裡，但是手搖飲料店家們在某些程度上懂得要如何操控消費者。」
- **加入譬喻和嘲諷**，在 Instagram 上上傳過時飲品的照片的話，人們會想到你到底是住在哪個星球上。
- 推論出，飲料公司就是意識到這點，所以操控奏效。

Step 2

- **主題是糖分攝取而非手搖飲**，故次段要拉回主題，並指出「因為青少年和年輕人是主要的購買族群，健康專家們對於現今糖尿病在這些族群中更為普遍的趨勢感到擔憂。」

Step 3

- 下個段落以醫生和教授的警告接續闡述，最終得出的結論是會影響孩童的學習表現。
- 直指這樣的購買行為會成為習慣，進一步以「腦部會傳遞訊息」讓你覺得有購買需要以得到滿足感接續陳述。
- 說明衍伸出的問題，「當手搖飲已經跟智慧型手機的使用有關聯時，就成了更為複雜的問題了。儘管健康專家和行為科學家兩者所做的努力，人們仍舊會出於新奇感而做出購買行為。」

Step 4

- 最後簡單地總結。

整合能力強化 ❹ 參考範文 ▶ *MP3 014*

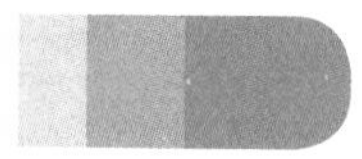

經由先前的演練後，現在請看整篇範文並聆聽音檔

New brands of the tea shake outlets are constantly popping up in the already saturated markets, but they somehow understand how to manipulate buyers. Uploading the picture of the old-fashioned drinks on the Instagram, people think what planet do you live on. Beverage companies are fully aware of this phenomenon, especially in today's society. Normally, people carry a smartphone with them, and most with the Instagram installed. They check new messages every now and then whenever they have the time. **The manipulation works exceedingly well, although some creative flavors of the drink do not make customers glued to the store.**

新品牌的手搖飲料店如雨後春筍般不斷地浮現在已經飽和的市場裡，但是手搖飲料店家們在某些程度上懂得要如何操控消費者。在 Instagram 上上傳過時飲品的照片的話，人們會想到你是住在哪個星球上。飲料公司完全意識到這個現象，特別是在現今的社會裡。通常，人們都會隨身攜帶智慧型手機，且手機上會安裝好 Instagram。每當他們有閒暇時間的時候，就會偶爾檢視下新訊息。儘管有些創意風味的飲料並未讓顧客欲罷不能，這樣的操控卻出奇地奏效。

Whether these drinks are genuinely scrumptious, our health has been greatly influenced by those hand-shaken drinks, leading us to rethink about the consumption of sugar in a day. Health experts are worried that diabetes is bound to be more prevalent among today's teenagers and young people since they are the main purchasers.

不論這些飲料是否真的美味出奇，我們的健康都受到這些手搖飲大幅地影響了，導致我們重新思考著每日所攝取的糖分。因為青少年和年輕人是主要的購買族群，健康專家們對於現今糖尿病在這些族群中更為普遍的趨勢感到擔憂。

Doctors and college professors are warning parents of the grisliness of consuming too much sugar because children's cognitive development may be worsened. The result is a poor performance reflected on kids' academic reports. The problem with these drinks is that it will be a routine. Regardless of age, people will form the habit of purchasing the drink. When you are not having the drink during the lunch time at work or after school, you feel an odd sense of eccentricity. Your brain signals a message that you have to buy a drink to feel satisfied, although some just want a drink to please Instagram followers. When the hand-shaken drinks have been linked with the use of smartphone, it has become an even more complicated problem. Despite the effort made by both Health experts and behavior scientists, still people are making the purchase out of a novelty.

醫生和大學教授都警告父母攝取過多的糖分的嚴重性，因為孩童的認知發展可能會因此而惡化。結果就是反應在孩童的學術成績單上面，學習表現不佳。問題是這些飲料會讓其成為常規。不分年齡，人們會有購買飲料的習慣。在下課或午餐期間，你沒有購買飲料的話，你會有奇怪的感覺。你的腦部會傳遞訊息給你，讓你覺得必須要購買飲料以覺得滿足，儘管有些人購買飲料只是要迎合 Instagram 的追蹤者。當手搖飲已經跟智慧型手機的使用有關聯時，就成了更為複雜的問題了。儘管健康專家和行為科學家兩者所做的努力，人們仍舊會出於新奇感而做出購買行為。

To sum up, unless people have an unwavering mindset and have formed the habit of drinking water or healthy beverages, hand-shaken drinks, like those cockroaches, will always be found in the kitchen, and will never be got rid of.

總之，除非人們有無可動搖的心態且已經有了飲用水或健康飲料的習慣，手搖飲就像那些總是會出現在廚房中的蟑螂一樣，是永遠無法根除的。

UNIT 08

無人駕駛汽車不是個新的概念了。許多民眾也已經在新聞上看過了類似的廣告。民眾對這個發明看法兩極，而你的看法又是什麼呢？請提出具體的例子解釋。

Writing Task 2

TOPIC

Driverless cars are not a new concept. Many people have seen similar ads from the news, but people's perception on driverless cars is varied. Some criticize, whereas others are welcoming them in the open arms? What is your viewpoint on this? Use specific examples to elucidate the phenomenon.

Write at least 250 words

整合能力強化 ❶ 實際演練

請搭配左頁的題目和並構思和完成大作文的演練。

整合能力強化 ❷ 單句中譯英演練

❶ 從鼓勵你購買安全程級為等級二的無人駕駛汽車的廣告，到嘲諷一些尚未購買最新上市、等級三的無人駕駛汽車的視頻，究竟為什麼我們必須要花費那麼多的關注在無人駕駛汽車這個議題上頭？

____

____

【參考答案】

From the car advert encouraging you to purchase a safe Level 2 driverless cars to a video that derides someone for not yet shopping the latest Level 3 driverless cars, why on earth do we have to pay lots of attention on the issue of driverless cars?

❷ 有些人聲稱無人駕駛汽車會主導未來的交通系統，而且駕駛無人駕駛汽車的利大於弊。

____

____

【參考答案】

Some proclaim that driverless cars will dominate the future traffic system, and benefits of driving driverless cars outweigh the disadvantages.

❸ 在一些交通事故佔據新聞頭條後，其他人則講述，如果執行不當的話，無人駕駛汽車會是雙面刃。

【參考答案】

Others, after some traffic accidents having taken up the news headlines, say that driverless cars are a double-edged sword, if poorly implemented.

❹ 在新聞文章中，甚至述說著無人駕駛汽車可能會錯誤評判交通號誌，對用路安全造成危險。

【參考答案】

In the news article, it even states the fact that driverless cars might misinterpret traffic signs, posing hazards to road safety.

❺ 事實上，無人駕駛汽車提供我們千變萬化的益處，特別是在經濟蕭條和物價通膨的時候。首先，無人駕駛汽車會帶來許多財政優勢。

【參考答案】

In fact, driverless cars provide us with kaleidoscopic benefits, especially during the economic downturn and price inflations. First, applications of driverless cars will bring a lot of financial benefits.

❻ 第二，自動駕駛汽車會降低由疲勞、緊張、疾病和其他因素引起的人為失誤。

【參考答案】
Second, autonomous cars will reduce human errors, which are caused by fatigue, nervousness, diseases, and other factors.

❼ 第三，對於那些行動不便者，無人駕駛汽車實際上會是個福音，因為他們無法駕駛汽車。

【參考答案】
Third, for those with disability, driverless cars are actually a blessing, since they are unable to drive.

❽ 行動不便者不需要仰賴其他人替他們開車。

【參考答案】
They do not have to depend on others to drive the car for them.

❾ 第五，對環境來說是有益處的，因為無人駕駛汽車使用電和電池。環境汙染會大幅減少。全球暖化的問題也會微幅受到控制。

【參考答案】

Fifth, it will be good for the environment because driverless cars use electricity and batteries. Environmental pollution will be greatly reduced. Global warming problems will be slightly under control.

⑩ 最後，對於需要長期駕駛的人來說，無人駕駛汽車可以讓那些人免受此苦。

【參考答案】

Finally, for people who drive for longer periods of time, driverless cars can save those people from misery.

整合能力強化 ❸ 段落拓展

TOPIC

Driverless cars are not a new concept. Many people have seen similar ads from the news, but people's perception on driverless cars is varied. Some criticize, whereas others are welcoming them in the open arms? What is your viewpoint on this? Use specific examples to elucidate the phenomenon.

Step 1 ■ 從現實生活中的廣告和視頻導入主題，最後反思「究竟為什麼我們必須要花費那麼多的關注在無人駕駛汽車這個議題上頭？」

Step 2 ■ 用 some 和 others 分別介紹無人駕駛汽車/自動駕車的利弊。

■ 在反面部分，強化提到「如果執行不當的話，無人駕駛汽車會是雙面刃。」以及「在新聞文章中，甚至述說著無人駕駛汽車可能會錯誤評判交通號誌，對用路安全造成危險。」

Step 3 ■ 用 listing patterns，列舉優點。

✧無人駕駛汽車會帶來許多財政優勢。

✧自動駕駛汽車會降低由疲勞、緊張、疾病和其他因素引起的人為失誤。

✧對於那些行動不便者，無人駕駛汽車實際上會是個福音，因為他們無法駕駛汽車。

✧對環境來說是有益處的，因為無人駕駛汽車使用電和電池。環境汙染會大幅減少。全球暖化的問題也會微幅受到控制。

✧對於需要長期駕駛的人來說，無人駕駛汽車可以讓那些人免受此苦。

Step 4 ■ 簡短地總結。

 整合能力強化 ❹ 參考範文 ▶ *MP3 015* 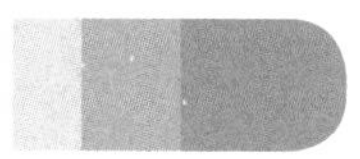

經由先前的演練後，現在請看整篇範文並聆聽音檔

From the car advert encouraging you to purchase a safe Level 2 driverless cars to a video that derides someone for not yet shopping the latest Level 3 driverless cars, why on earth do we have to pay lots of attention on the issue of driverless cars?

從鼓勵你購買安全程級為等級二的無人駕駛汽車的廣告，到嘲諷一些尚未購買最新上市、等級三的無人駕駛汽車的視頻，究竟為什麼我們必須要花費那麼多的關注在無人駕駛汽車這個議題上頭？

Some proclaim that driverless cars will dominate the future traffic system, and benefits of driving driverless cars outweigh the disadvantages. **Others, after some traffic accidents having taken up the news headlines, say that driverless cars are a double-edged sword, if poorly implemented.** In the news article, it even states the fact that driverless cars might misinterpret traffic signs, posing hazards to road safety.

有些人聲稱無人駕駛汽車會主導未來的交通系統，而且駕駛無人駕駛汽車的利大於弊。在一些交通事故佔據新聞頭條後，其他人則講述，如果執行不當的話，無人駕駛汽車會是雙面刃。在新聞文章中，甚至述說著無人駕駛汽車可能會錯誤評判交通號誌，對用路安全造成危險。

In fact, driverless cars provide us with kaleidoscopic benefits, especially during the economic downturn and price inflations. First, applications of driverless cars will bring a lot of financial benefits. Second, autonomous cars will reduce human errors, which are caused by fatigue, nervousness, diseases, and other factors. Third, for those with disability, driverless cars are actually a blessing, since they are unable to drive. They do not have to depend on others to drive the car for them. Fourth, it will increase overall efficiency, so there will not be traffic congestions. Fifth, it will be good for the environment because driverless cars use electricity and batteries. Environmental pollution will be greatly reduced.

Global warming problems will be slightly under control. Finally, for people who drive for longer periods of time, driverless cars can save those people from misery.

事實上，無人駕駛汽車提供我們千變萬化的益處，特別是在經濟蕭條和物價通膨的時候。首先，無人駕駛汽車會帶來許多財政優勢。第二，自動駕駛汽車會降低由疲勞、緊張、疾病和其他因素引起的人為失誤。第三，對於那些行動不便者，無人駕駛汽車實際上會是個福音，因為他們無法駕駛汽車。行動不便者不需要仰賴其他人替他們開車。第四，會增進整體效率，這樣一來就不會有交通壅擠的問題存在。第五，對環境來說是有益處的，因為無人駕駛汽車使用電和電池。環境汙染會大幅減少。全球暖化的問題也會微幅受到控制。最後，對於需要長期駕駛的人來說，無人駕駛汽車可以讓那些人免受此苦。

To sum up, despite the fact that it remains long to see whether or not driverless cars will be prevalent, I do think the benefits outweigh the disadvantages.

總之，儘管無人駕駛汽車是否會普及仍有待時間證明，我確實認為這是利大於弊的。

NOTE

UNIT 01 畢業後面臨就業，你會選擇「藍領工作」還是「白領工作」，為什麼呢？

Writing Task 2

TOPIC

Nowadays, lower wages are prevalent among younger generations, and statistics has shown that blue collar jobs offer job applicants significantly higher salaries than white collar jobs. However, it seems that higher salaries are not the top concern among graduates because there are other considerations. Which job will you choose, a blue collar job or a white collar job? Use specific examples and give your opinion.

Write at least 250 words

整合能力強化 ❶ 實際演練

請搭配左頁的題目和並構思和完成大作文的演練。

整合能力強化 ❷ 單句中譯英演練

❶ 根據統計，許多人選擇了白領的工作而非選擇藍領的工作，即使相較之下，藍領工作的薪資比起白領工作更高。

【參考答案】

According to the statistics, lots of people are choosing white-collar jobs instead of picking blue-collar jobs, even if comparatively the salary of the blue-collar jobs is much higher than that of white collar jobs.

❷ 所進行的調查結果並沒有令許多專家和學者們感到驚訝，因為藍領工作牽涉到許多艱困的工作和勞力。

【參考答案】

The survey conducted does not astound many experts and scholars since blue-collar jobs involve some arduous work and labor.

❸ 不像較年長的世代那樣以利字當頭並且會願意從事任何工作，較年輕的世代將乾淨和舒適感擺得比薪資更為重要。

【參考答案】
Younger generations, unlike older generations, who will do whatever it takes as long as the benefit outweighs the other, put the cleanliness and comfort much ahead of the salary.

❹ 上述的陳述可能並非以精準的方式去呈現兩方的立場，但是你越早工作，你越能了解到你所喜歡從事的工作。

____

____

【參考答案】
The above statements might not be an accurate way to present both sides, but the earlier you work, the earlier you will figure out what you like to do.

❺ 有些白領工作者，在公司工作幾年後，最終了解到藍領工作才是他們嚮往的。

____

____

【參考答案】
Some white-collar workers after working in the office for a few years, eventually figure out that blue-collar jobs are what they fancy.

❻ 其他人像是傑瑞・卡布納里在《第一份工作》中最終了解到藍領工作不是一份他將來想從事的工作，在他具有芝加哥的魚公司工作經驗後。

【參考答案】

Others like Jerry Carbonari in "*First Jobs*" eventually figures out the blue-collar job is not the job that he will be doing after his job experiences in a fish company in Chicago.

❼ 依我來看，我在高中時已經從事了許多的藍領工作。對於那些工作沒有任何浪漫情節在了。

【參考答案】

In my opinion, I have done lots of blue-collar jobs in high school. There was not any romance in such jobs.

❽ 所有那個時期所從事的工作都需要你從事艱苦和耗費勞力的工作，而且即使是不需要耗費體力活的工作，它磨掉了你的耐心。

【參考答案】

All require you to do arduous and strenuous work, and even if it is not something that needs physical work, it wears off your patience.

❾ 最重要的是，當你還相當年輕時，你的身體可以承受那樣的殘酷和工作量，但是當你漸漸年長後，你很難從事那樣的工作。

【參考答案】

Most important of all, when you are really young, your body can afford such cruelty and workload, but when you are getting older, it is highly unlikely for you to do such a job.

❿ 而且，你沒有辦法從工作中累積工作經驗，因為你只是不斷重複做同樣的事情。在大部分的藍領工作做十年後，對於雇主來說是無足輕重的，但是當你在從事特定的白領工作時，你能夠累積你的工作經驗。

【參考答案】

Also, you are not going to accumulate work experiences because you are doing the same thing over and over. Ten years of working in most blue-collar jobs will mean nothing to employers in other companies, but when you are doing certain white-collar jobs, you can accumulate your work experiences.

整合能力強化 ❸ 段落拓展

TOPIC

Nowadays, lower wages are prevalent among younger generations, and statistics has shown that blue collar jobs offer job applicants significantly higher salaries than white collar jobs. However, it seems that higher salaries are not the top concern among graduates because there are other considerations. Which job will you choose, a blue collar job or a white collar job? Use specific examples and give your opinion.

搭配的暢銷書

- *First Jobs*《第一份工作》

Step 1 題目是詢問關於兩種類型的工作：在白領工作和藍領工作中的選擇。首段以清楚且流暢的表達來呈現，包含兩者間的比較，並談到兩個世代在選擇上的不同，最後以年輕世代的考量點（乾淨和舒適感）作結尾。

Step 2 次個段落，除了延續上個段落的陳述外，包含了工作者在工作選擇上的改變，由白領到藍領（代表年輕世代並非都會持續選擇白領工作）。接續以暢銷書《第一份工作》進行論述，作者在芝加哥的魚公司工作體驗後，更了解自己想要什麼，進而不想選擇藍領工作。（確實有實際的工作體驗後，更能協助了解自我，而各種因素都影響了一個人選擇藍領或白領工作，也代表並沒有絕對要選擇哪樣的工作，這個並無是非對錯）。

Step 3 末段拉回自己本身的工作體驗，當中描述到藍領工作的辛苦處等等，**最主要的論點是放在為什麼選擇藍領或白領工作，範文中選擇的論點是會想選擇「白領工作」，必須要有支持這方面的特點或原因在**，文中也陸續提到了，藍領工作很難累積工作經驗，因為工作的重複性太高，也代表取代性高，另一方面是這是勞力工作，在年輕時體力能夠負擔，但是之後卻不見得能夠如此。

Step 4 經由前幾個段落的論述後，末段表明出自己仍會選擇白領工作。

整合能力強化 ❹ 參考範文 ▶ *MP3 016*

經由先前的演練後，現在請看整篇範文並聆聽音檔

According to the statistics, lots of people are still choosing white-collar jobs instead of picking blue-collar jobs, even if comparatively the salary of the blue-collar jobs is much higher than that of white-collar jobs. The survey conducted does not astound many experts and scholars since blue-collar jobs involve some arduous work and labor. Younger generations, unlike older generations, who will do whatever it takes as long as the benefit outweighs the other, put the cleanliness and comfort much ahead of the salary.

根據統計，即使相較之下，藍領工作者的薪資比起白領工作更高，許多人仍選擇了白領工作而非藍領工作。所進行的調查結果並沒有令許多專家和學者們感到驚訝，因為藍領工作牽涉到許多艱困的工作和勞力。不像較年長的世代那樣以利字當頭並且會願意從事任何工作，較年輕的世代將乾淨和舒適感擺得比薪資更為重要。

The above-mentioned statements might not be an accurate way to present both sides, but the earlier you work, the earlier you will figure out what you like to do. Some white-collar workers after working in the office for a few years, eventually figure out that blue-collar jobs are what they fancy. Others like Jerry Carbonari in "*First Jobs*" eventually figures out the blue-collar job is not the job that he will be doing after his job experiences in a fish company in Chicago. Of course, there are no right or wrong answers when it comes to choosing the job.

以上所提到的陳述可能並非以精準的方式去呈現兩方的立場，但是你若越早工作，你越能了解到你所喜歡從事的工作。在公司工作幾年後，有些白領工作者，最終了解到藍領工作才是他們嚮往的。在《第一份工作》中，其他像是傑瑞・卡布納里，在具有芝加哥的魚公司工作經驗後，最終了解到藍領工作不是一份他將來想從事的工作。當然，當提到選擇工作時，沒有所謂的對或錯的答案。

In my opinion, I have done lots of blue-collar jobs in high school. There was not any romance in such jobs. All require you to do arduous and strenuous work, and even if it is not something that needs physical work, it wears off your patience. All jobs are repetitive and after those experiences I admire blue-collar workers even more. Those jobs do involve labors and you cannot have any voice. No one would do such a job and people doing those jobs are really for a living.

依我來看，我在高中時已經從事了許多的藍領工作。對於那些工作已經沒有任何浪漫情節在了。所有那個時期所從事的工作都需要你從事艱苦和耗費勞力的工作，而且即使是不需要耗費體力活的工作，它磨掉了你的耐心。所有工作都是重複性質的，而在具有那些工作經驗後，我更欽佩藍領工作者。那些工作牽涉到勞力，以及你不能有任何想法。沒人會想從事那樣的工作，而且人們做那些工作通常是為了生活。

Most important of all, when you are really young, your body can afford such cruelty and workload, but when you are getting older, it is highly unlikely for you to do such a job. Also, you are not going to accumulate work experiences because you are doing the same thing over and over. Ten years of working in most blue-collar jobs will mean nothing to employers in other companies, but when you are doing certain white-collar jobs, you can accumulate your work experiences. You make a job hop after working in the company for 3-5 years, and you are getting a new job title or even get a managerial position that makes your pay double.

最重要的是，當你還相當年輕時，你的身體可以承受那樣的殘酷和工作量，但是當你年紀漸長後，你很難從事那樣的工作。而且，你無法從工作中累積工作經驗，因為你只是不斷地重複做同樣的事情。在大部分的藍領工作做十年後，對於雇主來說是無足輕重的，但是當你在從事特定的白領工作時，你能夠累積你的工作經驗。你能夠在公司工作 3 到 5 年後轉職，而且你能獲得新的工作頭銜或是甚至獲取能使你工作薪資兩倍的管理工作。

To sum up, for all these reasons, I think I will choose a white-collar job right after I graduate.

總之，基於這些理由，我認為我在畢業後會選擇白領工作。

UNIT 02 工作中常會遇到的問題，「金錢」和「夢想」只能二選一，你又會如何抉擇呢？

Writing Task 2

TOPIC

In life, there are multiple dilemmas, and one of the biggest is choosing between money and dream. Some choose a job that offers a much higher salary, while others pick the job they love, but come with price of getting minimum wages. Sometimes reality is so cruel that it keeps multiple graduates from pursuing their dreams. Do you think people should pursue their dreams or should they pursue money? Use specific examples and explain.

Write at least 250 words

整合能力強化 ❶ 實際演練

請搭配左頁的題目和並構思和完成大作文的演練。

❶ 大多數畢業生對於他們是否該選擇較高薪的工作，還是該追求他們理想的工作，但卻僅能提供他們微薄薪資有著進退兩難的困境。

____

____

【參考答案】

Most graduates have the dilemma of whether they should choose a job that has a much higher salary or whether they should pursue their ideal job that only gives them meager paycheck.

❷ 這是對於許多 20 多歲的人的困境，他們不具工作經驗或僅有些許工作經驗。

____

____

【參考答案】

It is the predicament for many twentysomethings who have zero work experiences or have little work experiences.

❸ 也千真萬確的是，他們大多數的人大學畢業後，從事著與他們本科系全然無關的工作。

____

____

【參考答案】

It is also true that most of them graduating out of the university doing jobs totally unrelated to their majors.

❹ 有些最終獲取工作成了房地產經紀人賺取大把鈔票。即使他們有些人賺取比他們同儕更多的金錢，像是這樣的問題縈繞在他們心中，尤其是當他們獨自一人時。

____

____

【參考答案】

Some eventually get the job as realtors earning lots of money. Even if some of them are earning more money than their peers, questions like these linger in their minds, especially when they are alone.

❺ 其他人賺了很多錢，但是最終辭掉了他們的工作，追求他們真正所愛的工作。

____

____

【參考答案】

Others are earning lots of money, but eventually quit their jobs by pursuing what they truly love.

❻ 當然，對於此決定沒有所謂的對或錯的答案。人們對於年薪賺超過一百萬台幣的人的評論大不相同。

【參考答案】

Of course, there are no right or wrong answers to this. Comments about people earning more a million NT dollars a year vary.

❼ 有的人替他們辯護，藉由述說著他們做對的事情。有些工作確實需要你做幾個轉換而且有相當重的工作量。

【參考答案】

Others defend them by saying that they are doing the right thing. Some jobs do require you to make several shifts and have a heavy workload.

❽ 最後，這確實對於他們的健康造成了很大的傷害。既然健康比起財富來說更為重要，他們之所以辭掉工作也是合理的。還有其他人辭掉工作是因為他們對於他們所從事的工作並沒有感到熱情。

【參考答案】
Eventually, it does take a toll on their health. Since health is above wealth, they are reasonable enough to quit. Still others quit the jobs because they are not passionate about what they are doing.

❾ 這像是在浪費他們的生命。對於所從事的工作不是你所熱愛的是很難維持下去的。在《你如何衡量你的人生》，它述說到「唯一使你真的感到滿足是從事你認為是偉大的工作，而唯一能做出驚人之作是要喜愛你所從事的。」

____

____

【參考答案】
It's like they are wasting their life. It is hard to sustain the effort doing things that are not what you love. In *How Will You Measure Your Life*, it states the fact that "The only way to be truly satisfied is to do what you believe is great work. And the only way to do great work is to love what you do."

❿ 賈伯斯確實預見了 20 幾歲的人和 30 幾歲的人所遭遇到的進退兩難的困境。

____

____

【參考答案】
Steve Jobs certainly foresees the dilemma that twentysomethings and thirtysomethings encounter.

整合能力強化 ❸ 段落拓展

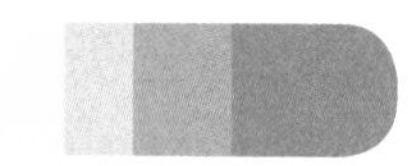

TOPIC

In life, there are multiple dilemmas, and one of the biggest is choosing between money and dream. Some choose a job that offers a much higher salary, while others pick the job they love, but come with price of getting minimum wages. Sometimes reality is so cruel that it keeps multiple graduates from pursuing their dreams. Do you think people should pursue their dreams or should they pursue money? Use specific examples and explain.

搭配的暢銷書

- *How Will You Measure Your Life*《你如何衡量你的人生》
- *Where You Go Is Not Who You Will B*e《你所讀的學校並非你能成為什麼樣的人》

Step 1 這題提到的關於理想和金錢的選擇。先定義了大學畢業生的困境（追求理想等同要放棄許多，甚至獲取更低的薪資，影響生活品質等），緊接著提到了從事與本科系無關的工作。例子中提到了從事房地產經紀人賺取大把鈔票，但終究不長久，有許多人後來還是辭掉這些高薪工作。

Step 2 次段提到了幾個論述，並推論出「還有其他人辭掉工作是因為他們對於他們所從事的工作並沒有感到熱情。」這是一個關鍵點。進一步以暢銷書《你如何衡量你的人生》的論點點出這是 20 幾歲的人和 30 幾歲的人所遭遇到的進退兩難的困境。

Step 3 末段提到了，金錢的流逝速度。並以暢銷書《你所讀的學校並非你能成為什麼樣的人》，它說到「你將會了解到如何賺錢，一旦你了解自己所愛的是什麼」。它提到了很重要的論點。最後以「擇你所愛」並對你來說是有價值的才是更重要的。

整合能力強化 ❹ 參考範文 ▶ *MP3 017*

經由先前的演練後，現在請看整篇範文並聆聽音檔

Most graduates have the dilemma of whether they should choose a job that has a much higher salary or whether they should pursue their ideal job that only gives them meager paycheck. It is the predicament for many twentysomethings who have zero work experiences or have little work experiences. It is also true that most of them graduating out of the university doing jobs totally unrelated to their majors. Some eventually get the job as realtors earning lots of money. Even if some of them are earning more money than their peers, questions like these linger in their minds, especially when they are alone. Others are earning lots of money, but eventually quit their jobs by pursuing what they truly love.

大多數的畢業生對於他們是否該選擇較高薪的工作，還是該追求僅能提供他們微薄薪資但卻是他們心中理想的工作，有著進退兩難的困境。這是對於許多 20 多歲的人的困境，他們不具工作經驗或僅有些許工作經驗。也千真萬確的是，他們大多數的人大學畢業後，從事著與他們本科系全然無關的工作。有些最終獲取工作成了房地產經紀人賺取大把鈔票。即使他們有些人賺取比他們同儕更多的金錢，像是這樣的問題仍縈繞在他們心中，尤其是當他們獨自一人時。其他人賺取了很多錢，但是最終辭掉了他們的工作，追求他們真正所愛的工作。

Of course, there are no right or wrong answers to this. Comments about people earning more a million NT dollars a year vary. Some say they are insane because they quit their jobs. Others defend them by saying that they are doing the right thing. Some jobs do require you to make several shifts and have a heavy workload. Eventually, it does take a toll on their health.

當然，對於此決定沒有所謂的對或錯的答案。人們對於年薪賺超過一百萬台幣者的評論大不相同。有的人替他們辯護，藉由述說著他們是在做對的事情。有些工作確實需要你做幾個轉換而且有相當繁重的工作量。最後，這確實對於他們的健康造成了很大的傷害。

Since health is above wealth, quitting the job seems reasonable enough. Still others quit the jobs because they are not passionate about what they are doing. It's like they are wasting their life. It is hard to sustain the effort doing things that are not what you love. In *How Will You Measure Your Life*, it states the fact that **"The only way to be truly satisfied is to do what you believe is great work. And the only way to do great work is to love what you do."** Steve Jobs certainly foresees the dilemma that twentysomethings and thirtysomethings might encounter.

既然健康比起財富來說更為重要，他們之所以辭掉工作也是合理的。還有其他人辭掉工作是因為他們對於所從事的工作並不具有熱情。這像是在浪費他們的生命。所從事的工作若不是你所熱愛的是很難維持下去的。在《你如何衡量你的人生》，它述說到「唯一使你真的感到滿足是從事你認為是偉大的工作，而唯一能做出驚人之作是要喜愛你所從事的。」賈伯斯確實預見了 20 幾歲的人和 30 幾歲的人可能遭遇到的進退兩難的困境。

Furthermore, money comes and goes very quickly. It is true that those realtors make a lot of money in a few years, but they also lose it in a quick fashion. In *Where You Go Is Not Who You Will Be*, it says **"you'll figure out how to make money once you figure out what you love to do."** People who choose to do what they truly love by quitting the job of a million NT dollars later are more successful than before. To sum up, we should really focus on the long-term rather on the short-term. High salaries may give us an immediate benefit, but life is long. Doing what you love and what really has values to you is more important.

此外，金錢來的快去得也快。千真萬確的是，那些房地產經理人在幾年內賺取了許多錢，但是他們也以很快的方式讓金錢流失掉。在《你所讀的學校並非你能成為什麼樣的人》中，它說到「你將會了解到如何賺錢，一旦你了解自己所愛的是什麼」。人們選擇了他們真的所愛的事情，進而辭掉了百萬年薪的工作，最終卻比先前更加成功。總之，我們應該要將重心放長遠，而非短期上。高薪可能給予我們立即的益處，但是人生是長久的。「擇你所愛」並對你來說是有價值的才是更重要的。

UNIT 03 工作中也會面臨在「累積經驗」和「獲取更多金錢」的抉擇，如果同時錄取兩間都是不錯的公司，又該如何選擇呢？

Writing Task 2

TOPIC

Although it is quite unlikely to happen in real life, it does happen sometimes. And what if you get two fantastic offers, one actually gives you an exceedingly high salary, while another can offer you the chance to grow but with a much lower salary. What decision will you make? Choosing money over experience or picking experience over money. Use specific examples and explain.

Write at least 250 words

整合能力強化 ❶ 實際演練

請搭配左頁的題目和並構思和完成大作文的演練。

❶ 獲取兩份很棒的工作錄取通知對於求職候選人來說絕對是很大的喜悅，但是知道如何選擇哪份工作更適合自己是數百萬的畢業生所面臨的困境。

【參考答案】

Getting two fantastic job offers is absolutely a great joy for the job candidates, but knowing how to choose which one is more suitable for you is the dilemma for millions of graduates.

❷ 如果 A 公司提供的金錢遠高於 B 公司，而 B 公司卻能滋養你，提供你所需要的經驗，你也能於接下來的 10 年茁壯成長，那麼你會如何做出選擇呢？

【參考答案】

If company A offers significantly more money than company B, whereas company B can nourish you with the experience necessary for you to be robust enough for the next 10 years, then what would you choose.

❸ 那麼，這已經成了在經驗和金錢中做出選擇的問題了。

____

____

【參考答案】
Then it has become the question of choosing between experience and money.

❹ 甚至多 5000 元台幣對大學畢業生來說很多，因為這意謂著一年多了六萬元的收入，你不需要是位擅長數學的專家去了解這點。

____

____

【參考答案】
Even earning NT 5,000 dollars more will mean so much for university graduates because that's 60,000 dollars more in a year, and you don't have to be an expert who is good at math to realize it.

❺ 有些人說當機會敲門時，你必須要抓住且在你 30 歲前累積最多的金錢。

____

____

【參考答案】
Some say that when opportunities knock on the door, you have got to grasp and accumulate the most money before you turn thirty.

❻ 其他人則是勸阻你別僅僅追求金錢，反而鼓勵你去珍惜經驗，這樣一來你就不會於稍後有所遺憾，而兩方的立場也都有些令人信服的點存在。

【參考答案】
Others discourage you from pursuing solely for money and encourage you to value the experience so that you won't regret later, and both parties have some valid points.

❼ 而 Lehman Brothers 在當時很龐大，而且它能夠提供相當高的薪資。其中一位作者的人生指導員，喬治・史丹登提供了他的洞察。

【參考答案】
And Lehman Brothers was huge at that time and it can offer considerably higher pay. One of the author's mentors, George Stanton offers his insight.

❽ 「在人生中，確實會有時期是你應該要選擇金錢大於經驗」，「但是做那樣的選擇時，是當利潤是更大時，當利潤是數百萬美元，而不是數千元」。這確實是個引導我們思考為什麼的好方式。

【參考答案】

"There actually will be times in life when you should choose money over experience", "but make that choice when the margin is much bigger, when the margin is millions of dollars, not thousand." It is actually a good way to lead us to think about why.

❾ 長遠來看，經驗比金錢還重要，而且當利潤很少時，你應該要選擇經驗。在找工作期間或轉職時，經驗法則總是一樣的。

____

____

【參考答案】

For the long term, experience is more important than money, and when the margin is very little, you should choose experience. During the job search or job hop, the rule is always the same.

❿ 你不會因為另一間公司提供你高於現在公司給的薪資兩千元就決定要跳槽到另一間公司。

____

____

【參考答案】

You do not make a job hop just because another company offers you NT 2,000 more dollars than the salary that the current company offers you.

整合能力強化 ❸ 段落拓展

TOPIC

Although it is quite unlikely to happen in real life, it does happen sometimes. And what if you get two fantastic offers, one actually gives you an exceedingly high salary, while another can offer you the chance to grow but with a much lower salary. What decision will you make? Choosing money over experience or picking experience over money. Use specific examples and explain.

搭配的暢銷書

- "*The Promise of the Pencil* : how an ordinary person can create an extraordinary change"《一支鉛筆的承諾：一位普通人如何能創造出驚人的改變》

Step 1 題目詢問到如果同時接獲兩個極佳的錄取通知時，該選擇什麼呢？這題是詢問在金錢和經驗中做出選擇，而太模糊或不具體的表達其實等同沒有表達且更難獲取 7 以上的成績。首段先定義，並以詼諧的字句結尾，「... 因為這意謂著一年多了六萬元的收入，你不需要是位擅長數學的專家去了解這點。」，但這也並不表明會選擇金錢的立場。

Step 2 次段很簡潔且流暢表明出兩方立場，論點看似都很令人信服。

Step 3 下一段以暢銷書《一支鉛筆的承諾：一位普通人如何能創造出驚人的改變》中的實例來講述提升說服力，作者的 mentor 喬丹提出的論點很棒，也很能引導我們去思考，因為經驗最終助益最大。

■（範文中沒提到的是，作者最後選擇 Bain 而非 Lehman Brothers，更令人難置信的是 Lehman Brothers 這樣的大公司後來破產了，作者不禁思考如果選擇該公司自己命運又會是如何呢？而當時他有些朋友也面臨長期失業，作者慶幸自己選擇了 Bain）

Step 4 末段提到，從長遠來看，經驗比金錢還重要，最後講述自己的立場，經由這些推論跟實例後，自己會選擇經驗而非金錢。

整合能力強化 ❹ 參考範文 ▶ MP3 018

經由先前的演練後，現在請看整篇範文並聆聽音檔

Of course, lots of us have doubts that this can't be happening, but in life you just never know because anything can happen. Getting two fantastic job offers is absolutely a great joy for the job candidates, but knowing how to choose which one is more suitable for you is the dilemma for millions of graduates. If company A offers significantly more money than company B, whereas company B can nourish you with the experience necessary for you to be robust enough for the next 10 years, then what would you choose. Then it has become the question of choosing between experience and money. Even earning NT 5,000 dollars more will mean so much for university graduates because that's 60,000 dollars more in a year, and you don't have to be an expert who is good at math to realize it.

當然，我們許多人之中對此抱持著存疑的態度，這不可能發生，但是在生命中，你就是參透，因為任何事都有可能發生。獲取兩份很棒的工作錄取通知對於求職候選人來說絕對是很大的喜悅，但是知道如何選擇哪份工作更適合自己是數百萬的畢業生所面臨的困境。如果 A 公司提供的金錢遠高於 B 公司，而 B 公司卻能滋養你，提供你所需要的經驗，你也能於接下來的 10 年中茁壯成長，那麼你會如何做出選擇呢？那麼，這已經成了在經驗和金錢中做出選擇的問題了。你不需要是位擅長數學的專家去了解這點，甚至多 5000 元台幣對大學畢業生來說很多了，因為這意謂著一年多了六萬元的收入。

The debate can go on and on. Some say that when opportunities knock on the door, you have got to grasp and accumulate the most money before you turn thirty. Others discourage you from pursuing solely for money and encourage you to value the experience so that you won't regret later, and both parties have some valid points.

辯論可以不斷持續著。有些人說當機會敲門時，你必須要抓住，而且在你 30 歲前累積最多的金錢。其他人則是勸阻你別僅僅追求金錢，反而鼓勵你去珍惜經驗，這樣一來你就不會於稍後有所遺憾，而兩方的立場也都有令人信服的點存在。

In "*The Promise of the Pencil* : how an ordinary person can create an extraordinary change" the author actually faces the predicament like this. Should he choose Bain or Lehman? And Lehman Brothers was huge at that time and it can offer considerably higher pay. One of the author's mentors, George Stanton offers his insight. "**There actually will be times in life when you should choose money over experience", "but make that choice when the margin is much bigger, when the margin is millions of dollars, not thousand.**" It is actually a good way to lead us to think about why.

在《一支鉛筆的承諾：一位普通人如何能創造出驚人的改變》，作者實際上面臨了像是這樣的困境。他應該要選擇 Bain 還是 Lehman 呢？而 Lehman Brothers 在當時很龐大，而且它能夠提供相當高的薪資。其中一位作者的人生導師，喬治・史丹登提供了他的洞察。「在人生中，確實會有時期是你應該要選擇金錢大於經驗」，「但是做那樣的選擇時，是當利潤是更大時，當利潤是數百萬美元，而不是數千元」。這確實是個引導我們思考當中原因的好方式。

For the long term, experience is more important than money, and when the margin is very little, you should choose experience. During the job search or job hop, the rule is always the same. You do not make a job hop just because another company offers you NT 2,000 dollars more than the salary that the current company offers you. The margin is too little. Instead, you stay in the current company, and after 3-5 years your experience is significantly more valuable, you make a job hop to another company and probably the managerial position. You earn more than that. To sum up, from the above mentioned descriptions, I would choose experience over money.

長遠來看，經驗比金錢還重要，而且當利潤很少時，你應該要選擇經驗。在找工作期間或轉職時，經驗法則總是一樣的。你不會因為另一間公司提供你高於現在公司給的薪資兩千元就決定要跳槽到另一間公司。利潤太些微了。取而代之的是，你應該要待在現在的公司，而在 3 至 5 年後，你的經驗遠具更多價值時，你跳槽到另一間公司，而這可能是管理職的職缺。你能夠賺取多於那金額的錢。總之，從上述的描述，我會選擇經驗大於金錢。

UNIT 04 個人特質影響一個人是否能獲取成功，而就「聰明」跟「大膽」而言，哪個特質更重要呢？

Writing Task 2

TOPIC

Traits can shape a person. Traits are important because they can determine whether a person can succeed or not, and there are so many characteristics, such as honesty, wisdom, cleverness, and boldness. If we narrow down the traits to two, boldness and smartness, do you think which one is more important than the other? Use specific examples and explain.

Write at least 250 words

整合能力強化 ❶ 實際演練

請搭配左頁的題目和並構思和完成大作文的演練。

整合能力強化 ❷ 單句中譯英演練

❶「通常在真實世界裡，反而是具膽識者獲得成功，而非聰明的人。」這句源於《富爸爸窮爸爸》的話，似乎完全回應了關於哪個特質更為重要的這個問題。

____

____

【參考答案】
"Often in the real world, it's not the smart who get ahead, but the bold." This quote from *Rich Dad Poor Dad* pretty much answers the question about which characteristic is more important.

❷ 在處理特定的任務時，聰明可能給人們確切的優勢進而佔上風，但是那些事情是很瑣碎的。

____

____

【參考答案】
Smartness might give people a certain edge to prevail in certain tasks, but those things are trivial.

❸ 在最後，終究歸咎於你是否足夠勇敢，進而採取特定的對策。即使你不具備某種程度的聰明，而實情是你願意跨越過舒適圈，並執行它。

【參考答案】

In the end, it all comes down to whether you are gallant enough to make a certain move. Even if you do not possess a certain level of smartness, the thing is you are willing to go beyond the comfort zone and do it.

❹ 聰明的人可能對於整件事情過度思考了，而聰明但不具備膽識的人仍停留在原地，甚至連一寸都聞風不動，而具膽識的人冒險進入了一個嶄新的領域，並且讓這些產生了很大程度的不同。

【參考答案】

Smart people might overthink about the whole thing, and smart people without the courage to do things are still in the same spot, not moving for even an inch, whereas bold people venture into a new territory and that makes a huge difference.

❺ 在《但願當我 20 歲時就知道的事》，它談到了「這個世界區分成，在等待別人的許可去做他們想要從事的事情，以及自己給予自己許可去做事情的人」。

【參考答案】

In *What I Wish I Knew When I was 20*, it talks about "The world is divided into people who wait for others to give them permission to do the things they want to do and people who grant themselves permission."

❻ 千真萬確的是大多數的人不敢邁出大膽之舉，而且他們正等待別人給予許可權，像是書中所描述的情況一樣。

【參考答案】

It is true that most people do not dare to make the bold move and they are waiting for the permission like what the book describes.

❼ 當人們質疑你如何能夠創立一間公司，因為你僅是個員工，聰明的人有點退縮了，並且仍舊待在原來的公司當個員工。

【參考答案】

When people are doubting how can you start a company because you are just an employee, smart people shrink for a bit and remain as the employee of the company.

❽ 他們沒有採取任何行動，而反觀具膽識的人卻不在乎其他人怎麼想的。這並不是說他們變得不理性了。

【參考答案】

They do not make the move, while bold people do not care what others think about. It is not that they are being irrational.

❾ 他們已經對於整件事情做出了評估，這樣一來他們就能夠採取行動了。即使他們還僅是員工，他們的膽識給予他們足夠的勇氣去做這件事情。

【參考答案】

They have evaluated the whole thing so that they make such a move. Even though they are just an employee, their boldness gives them enough courage to do it.

❿ 當面臨所有質疑時，它們的反應是為什麼不呢，我已經在這間公司五年了，而且我對於所有這些程序和許多重要的戰略性商業決策都很熟悉了。

【參考答案】

When faced with all the doubts, they are like why not, I have been in this company for 5 years and I have already familiar with all the procedures and many important strategic business decisions.

整合能力強化 ❸ 段落拓展

TOPIC

Traits can shape a person. Traits are important because they can determine whether a person can succeed or not, and there are so many characteristics, such as honesty, wisdom, cleverness, and boldness. If we narrow down the traits to two, boldness and smartness, do you think which one is more important than the other? Use specific examples and explain.

搭配的暢銷書

- *Rich Dad Poor Dad*《窮爸爸富爸爸》
- *What I Wish I Knew When I was 20*《但願當我 20 歲時就知道的事》

Step 1 這是關於個人特質的題目，其實是蠻靈活的考題，在口說或寫作中，有時候會出現，可以認真思考下哪些特質對自己而言是最重要的。但題目有限定在兩個特質的討論，所以要針對這兩個特質，選出一個適合的，範文中選了 boldness，如果你選擇 smartness 就可以想下相關搭配的點是什麼。首段很清楚的使用了暢銷書《富爸爸窮爸爸》破題。

Step 2 次段則討論兩種特點的優缺點，進一步推論出，如果沒有足夠勇氣邁開那步，就算再聰明也無法達到該目標。

Step 3 下個段落提到了另一本暢銷書《但願當我 20 歲時就知道的事》，而確實是如此，有太多的人需要有周遭的人認同並給予允許才敢做某些事情，但其他具有膽識者早就去執行了，這就是兩者間的差異。然後進一步說明了在公司裡兩種類型的人在累積的資歷後，具膽識者可能已經創立了一間公司了，對比差異處。

Step 4 末段總結出具膽識者更容易獲取成功，而接續以暢銷書《富爸爸窮爸爸》結尾。

整合能力強化 ❹ 參考範文 ▶ *MP3 019*

經由先前的演練後，現在請看整篇範文並聆聽音檔

"Often in the real world, it's not the smart who get ahead, but the bold." This quote from *Rich Dad Poor Dad* pretty much answers the question about which characteristic is more important. Boldness outshines smartness, but why?

「通常在真實世界裡，反而是具膽識者獲得成功，而不是聰明的人。」這句源於《富爸爸窮爸爸》的話，似乎完全回應了關於哪個特質更為重要的這個問題。膽識使聰明相形見拙，但是這又是為什麼呢？

Smartness might give people a certain edge to prevail in certain tasks, but those things are trivial. In the end, it all comes down to whether you are gallant enough to make a certain move. Even if you do not possess a certain level of smartness, the thing is you are willing to go beyond the comfort zone and do it. Smart people might overthink about the whole thing, and smart people without the courage to do things are still in the same spot, not moving for even an inch, whereas bold people venture into a new territory and that makes a huge difference.

在處理特定的任務時，聰明可能給人們確切的優勢進而佔上風，但是那些事情是很瑣碎的。在最後，終究歸咎於你是否足夠勇敢，進而採取特定的對策。即使你不具備某種程度的聰明，而實情是你願意跨越過舒適圈，並執行它。聰明的人可能對於整件事情過度思考了，而聰明但不具備膽識的人仍停留在原地，甚至連一寸都聞風不動，而具膽識的人冒險進入了一個嶄新的領域，並且讓這些產生了很大程度的不同。

In *What I Wish I Knew When I was 20*, it talks about **"The world is divided into people who wait for others to give them permission to do the things they want to do and people who grant themselves permission."** It is true that most people do not dare to make the bold move and they are waiting for the permission like what the book describes. Bold people, on the other hand, do not wait for the permission of others. They do not need any permission. When people are doubting how can you start a company because you are just an employee, smart people shrink for a bit and remain as the employee of the company. They do not make the move, while bold people do not care what others think about. It is not that they are being irrational. They have evaluated the whole thing so that they make such a move. Even though they are just an employee, their boldness gives them enough courage to do it. When faced with all the doubts, they are like why not, I have been in this company for 5 years and I have already familiar with all the procedures and many important strategic business decisions.

在《但願當我 20 歲時就知道的事》，它談到了「這個世界區分成，在等待別人的許可去做他們想要從事的事情，以及自己給予自己許可去做事情的人」。千真萬確的是，大多數的人不敢邁出大膽之舉，而且他們正等待別人給予許可權，像是書中所描述的情況一樣。大膽之人，另一方面，不等待其他人給予許可。他們不需要任何許可。當人們質疑你如何能夠創立一間公司，因為你僅是個員工，聰明的人有點退縮了，並且仍舊待在原來的公司當個員工。他們沒有採取任何行動，而反觀具膽識的人卻不在乎其他人怎麼想的。這並不是說他們變得不理性了。他們已經對於整件事情做出了評估，這樣一來他們就能夠採取行動了。即使他們還僅是員工，他們的膽識給予他們足夠的勇氣去做這件事情。當面臨所有質疑時，它們的反應是為什麼不去做呢？我已經在這間公司待五年了，而且我對於所有這些程序和許多重要的戰略性商業決策都很熟悉了。

There is no reason to stop just because someone has doubts. They are more likely to be successful in the long term, whereas smart people use their smartness in the same company earning the meager salary. Bold people, on the contrary, might start a company and be someone else's boss and earn lots of money. Of course, it comes with the risk. But just like what's in the *Rich Dad Poor Dad*, "Winners are not afraid of losing. But losers are." To sum up, from the above mentioned statements, I do think boldness outshines smartness.

沒有停下來的理由，難道僅因為一些人對這些事情有些質疑嗎？長遠來看，他們更可能獲取成功，而聰明的人運用了他們的聰明在同間公司賺取微薄的薪水。反觀，大膽的人可能開創了一間公司，而成了有些人的老闆了，並賺取許多錢。當然，伴隨而之的是風險。但是這就像是《富爸爸窮爸爸》中所說道的，「贏家不害怕輸，但是魯蛇卻怕」。總之，從以上的陳述，我認為大膽遠勝過聰明。

UNIT 05 「成長型思維模式」和「固定型思維模式」對人們的學習和獲取成功影響甚鉅，請以具體實例解釋兩者間的差異。

Writing Task 2

TOPIC

Our thinking matters to us, and it can make or break us. Some are thinking in a narrower way, and they are having a fastened way of thinking, the so-called the fixed mindset. Others have a more flexible thinking approach. They think failures are part of the process and they actually help us succeed in life. They belong to the growth mindset. Do you think people should all learn both ideas so they can have a more fulfilling life? use specific examples and explain.

Write at least 250 words

整合能力強化 ❶ 實際演練

請搭配左頁的題目和並構思和完成大作文的演練。

整合能力強化 ❷ 單句中譯英演練

❶ 當賈斯汀，《醜女貝蒂》裡的其中一位角色，拿到拒絕錄取通知信時，他告訴他的家人，他不想要等明年，以及他想要今年就要進他理想的學校就讀。

____

____

【參考答案】
When Justin, one of the characters in *Ugly Betty*, gets the rejection letter, he tells his family that he doesn't want next year, and he wants to go to his desired school this year.

❷ 他母親當時的男朋友，一位議員以簡單且值得讚許的方式回應了他這個舉動。

____

____

【參考答案】
How his mother's boyfriend, a senator, responds to his reaction, is simple but commendable.

❸ 他說這是需要時間的，而這也是為什麼要花費他數年，他才獲取現在的職位。

____

____

【參考答案】

He says it takes time, and this is why it takes him years to get his position now.

❹ 藉由分析他們對於挫折的反應，我們可以很清楚看到賈斯汀是位具有固定型思維模式的人，而議員卻具有成長型思維模式。

____

____

【參考答案】

By analyzing how they react to failures, we can clearly see that Justin is someone with a fixed mindset, whereas the senator possesses the growth mindset.

❺ 在《關鍵十年》，它也談論到成長型思維模式的重要性。「對於那些具有成長型思維模式者，失敗可能會讓人感到刺痛，但是他們將其視為是改進和改變的機會」。

____

____

【參考答案】

In *The Defining Decade*, it also talks about the importance of the growth mindset. “For those who have a growth mindset, failures may sting but they are also viewed as opportunities for improvement and change.”

❻ 在《我在工作中所犯的錯誤》，卡洛斯・德維克提及「當你具有成長型思維模式時，你了解到錯誤和挫折是學習中不可或缺的一部分」。

【參考答案】
In *Mistakes I Made at Work*, Carol S. Dweck mentions "When you have a "growth mindset", you understand that mistakes and setbacks are an inevitable part of learning."

❼ 兩者清楚地顯示出思考模式的重要性，以及這會如何影響到結果。

【參考答案】
Both clearly show the importance of thinking patterns and how it is going to affect the result.

❽ 具有固定型思維模式者，像是賈斯汀這樣的人，似乎無法好好處理挫折，而這或多或少衝擊他們稍後的表現。

【參考答案】

People possessing a fixed mindset, someone like Justin, cannot seem to handle rejections well, and this more or less impacts their later performance.

⑨ 因為失敗的經驗，它實際上幫助你修復你內在所欠缺的，而你如何能夠在進行第二次嘗試時，改進事情和做出更好的工作成果。

____

____

【參考答案】

Because of the failing experience, it actually helps you remedy what is clearly lacking inside you, and how you can improve things and do a better job in the second attempt.

⑩ 一旦你的思考模式已經從固定型思維模式轉換到成長型思維模式，你將發現，生活簡單多了，而成功總是近在咫呎。

____

____

【參考答案】

Once your thinking patterns have changed from a fixed mindset to a growth mindset, you will find life is a lot easier and success is always near.

TOPIC

Our thinking matters to us, and it can make or break us. Some are thinking in a narrower way, and they are having a fastened way of thinking, the so-called the fixed mindset. Others have a more flexible thinking approach. They think failures are part of the process and they actually help us succeed in life. They belong to the growth mindset. Do you think people should all learn both ideas so they can have a more fulfilling life? use specific examples and explain.

搭配的暢銷書

- *The Defining Decade*《關鍵十年》
- *Mistakes I Made at Work*《我在工作中所犯的錯誤》

Step 1 ■ 題目是關於兩種思維模式：成長型思維模式和固定型思維模式，常見的敘述手法較難寫出好的論點。首段以很引人入勝的手法切入，是上乘的佳作。藉由影集中人物帶入主題，而非一堆陳述句和定義，讓讀者能接續閱讀下去，並從影集中兩位人物比較出要介紹的兩的觀點，1 賈斯汀（fixed mindset）2 議員（Growth mindset）

Step 2 次段以另外兩本暢銷書解釋和定義這兩個思維模式的差異，是很具體的表達，從中可以很明顯的了解到思考模式影響到成果。**成長型思維模式者將其視為是改進和改變的機會，而且了解到錯誤和挫折是學習中不可或缺的一部分**，這也是他們更能成功的原因。

Step 3

- 下一段，經由上一段的解釋跟進一步的定義後，再回來談論剛剛兩位主角並做出總結，也是藉由比較得出結論，推論出你就具備了成功的特質，而且你不用因為失敗的嘗試被擊倒。

- 一旦你的思考模式已經從固定型思維模式轉換到成長型思維模式，你將發現，生活簡單多了，而成功總是近在咫呎。最後說明我們都該要對這兩個思考模式有認識，這對我們生活中有幫助。

整合能力強化 ❹ 參考範文 ▶ *MP3 020*

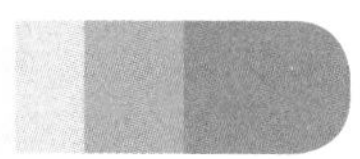

經由先前的演練後，現在請看整篇範文並聆聽音檔

When Justin, one of the characters in *Ugly Betty*, gets the rejection letter, he tells his family that he doesn't want next year, and he wants to go to his desired school this year. How his mother's boyfriend, a senator, responds to his reaction, is simple but commendable. He says it takes time, and this is why it takes him years to get his position now. By analyzing how they react to failures, we can clearly see that Justin is someone with a fixed mindset, whereas the senator possesses the growth mindset.

當賈斯汀，《醜女貝蒂》裡的其中一位角色，拿到錄取通知的拒絕信時，他告訴他的家人，他不想要等到明年，以及他想要今年就要進他理想的學校就讀。他母親當時的男朋友，一位議員以簡單且值得讚許的方式回應了他這個舉動。他說這是需要時間的，而這也是為什麼要花費他數年，他才獲取現在的職位。藉由分析他們對於挫折的反應，我們可以很清楚看到賈斯汀是位具有固定型思維模式的人，而議員卻具有成長型思維模式。

The two following bestsellers also discuss the concept of the growth mindset. In *The Defining Decade*, it also talks about the importance of the growth mindset. **"For those who have a growth mindset, failures may sting but they are also viewed as opportunities for improvement and change."** In *Mistakes I Made at Work*, Carol S. Dweck mentions **"When you have a "growth mindset", you understand that mistakes and setbacks are an inevitable part of learning."** Both clearly show the importance of thinking patterns and how it is going to affect the result.

下列兩位暢銷書作者也討論到了成長型思維模式的觀念。在《關鍵十年》，它也談論到成長型思維模式的重要性。「對於那些具有成長型思維模式者，失敗可能會讓人感到刺痛，但是他們將其視為是改進和改變的機會」。在《我在工作中所犯的錯誤》，卡洛斯・德維克提及「當你具有成長型思維模式時，你了解到錯誤和挫折是學習中不可或缺的一部分」。兩者清楚地顯示出思考模式的重要性，以及這會如何影響到結果。

People possessing a fixed mindset, someone like Justin, cannot seem to handle rejections well, and this more or less impacts their later performance. They can view things as this is too hard to accomplish, and the thinking pattern is set. They think they are never going to make it. But to people who have the growth mindset, they see things differently. They see things as something that really takes some time and effort to get there. They are not defeated at a first no, and in fact it is true that most people do not get the desired result in their first attempt. In life, you have to value failures as the nutrition for growth. Because of the failing experience, it actually helps you remedy what is clearly lacking inside you, and how you can improve things and do a better job in the second attempt. If you view things like this, you have possessed the quality for success, and you won't feel quashed by failed attempts. Once your thinking patterns have changed from a fixed mindset to a growth mindset, you will find life is a lot easier and success is always near.

像是賈斯汀這樣具有固定型思維模式的人，似乎無法好好處理挫折，而這或多或少衝擊他們稍後的表現。他們可以將事情看成難度過高而無法達成，而這樣的思考模式就定型了。他們認為自己無法達成。但是對於有著思考型思維模式者，他們看事情的角度卻是截然不同。他們把事情看成是一些真的需要時間和努力去達到。他們不會因為第一次的拒絕而被擊倒，而事實上，千真萬確的是，大多數的人並沒有在首次嘗試時就達到理想的結果。在生命中，你必須要將失敗當成是成長的養分。因為失敗的經驗，它實際上幫助你修復你內在所欠缺的，而你如何能夠在進行第二次嘗試時，改進事情和做出更好的工作成果。如果你把事情看成是這樣的話，你就具備了成功的特質，而且你不用因為失敗的嘗試被擊倒。一旦你的思考模式已經從固定型思維模式轉換到成長型思維模式，你將發現，生活簡單多了，而成功總是近在咫呎。

To sum up, from the above mentioned descriptions, I think we should really know the difference between a fixed mindset and a growth mindset so that we can have a more satisfying life.

總之，從上述的描述，我認為我們真的應該要知道固定型思維模式和成長型思維模式，這樣一來我們就可以有更滿足的生活。

UNIT 06

許多人嚮往能在工作和生活中取得平衡，是否有能取得工作和生活平衡的工作呢？如果有的話又要如何獲取這樣類型的工作呢？你認為思考的方式有影響嗎？

Writing Task 2

TOPIC

The idea of work-life balance is great, and lots of us have sought multiple approaches to get that, but to no avail. Do you think there are actually jobs that can meet the work-life balance criteria. If so what are those and how to get the kind of job. Do you think ways of thinking matter? Use specific examples and explain.

Write at least 250 words

整合能力強化 ❶ 實際演練

請搭配左頁的題目和並構思和完成大作文的演練。

整合能力強化 ❷ 單句中譯英演練

❶ 在《我工作中所犯的錯誤中》，金・古登提到「工作－生活平衡的想法並不總是有助益」。如果你沉浸在你的工作和養育一個家庭，你可能會感覺到許多好事情 – 但是可能不會包含平衡」。

___

___

【參考答案】

In *Mistakes I Made at Work*, Kim Gordon mentions "The idea of "work-life balance" is not necessarily helpful. If you are immersed in your work and raising a family, you might feel a lot of good things – but it may not include balanced."

❷ 這個陳述似乎是告知我們追求工作和生活平衡的工作是不可能的，而這是令人沮喪的。

___

___

【參考答案】

The statement seems to inform us that seeking a work-life balance job is so unlikely, and this is so discouraging.

❸ 另一位專家，一位高勝資深經理說道「你越是談論到工作和生活平衡，你越是創造出你想要解決的問題」。

【參考答案】
Another expert, a senior director at Goldman Sachs said "the more you talk about work-life balance, the more you create the problem that you want to solve."

❹ 這進一步地證實了，會有接踵而來的問題，當你找尋那樣的工作時。但是工作和生活中平衡的工作是否存在？

【參考答案】
This further validates there is going to be an ensuing problem when you seek this kind of job. But does the job of work-life balance not exist?

❺ 專家們已經告訴我們的確實是有些根據和洞察性的重點，但是不論專家們告訴我們什麼，工作和生活中取得平衡的工作確實存在著。

【參考答案】
What experts have told us do have some valid and insightful points, but regardless of what experts tell us, the job of work-life balance does exist.

❻ 這是夢幻工作，而非你追求而來的工作。這使我們大多數的人感到困惑。但這像是書中所述，夢幻工作通常是創造出來的，而非找到的。

____

____

【參考答案】
It is the dream job, and it is not something that you seek. This puzzles many of us. But it is like what is described in the book, dream job is often created than found.

❼ 通常，這不是在你找工作的頁面中會看到的。這可能是個替有些具有不可取代的專業技巧和工作經驗者所打造的，而招募者認為你可以是唯一一個可以做那個工作的人。

____

____

【參考答案】
Normally, it is not the job that you see on the job search pages. This could be the job for someone who has irreplaceable technical skills and job experiences, and recruiters deem you can be the one to do the job.

❽ 這份工作是一些具有能力，可能能夠達到公司未來目標者所設計的。這樣的工作是相當罕見的。

____

____

【參考答案】
The job is designed for someone who might have the skill to do things that can meet the future goals of the company. This kind of the job is exceptionally rare.

❾ 有些工作讓你有足夠的彈性，每周的特定幾天你可以經營好你的工作和家庭。

____

____

【參考答案】
Some jobs are flexible enough for you to work for certain days a week so that you can manage both your work and your family.

❿ 總之，我認為有著對的思考模式，你可以管理好生活和工作，即使你沒有夢幻工作。

____

____

【參考答案】
To sum up, I think with right thinking mindset, you can manage both life and work, even if you do not have the dream job.

整合能力強化 ❸ 段落拓展

TOPIC

The idea of work-life balance is great, and lots of us have sought multiple approaches to get that, but to no avail. Do you think there are actually jobs that can meet the work-life balance criteria. If so what are those and how to get the kind of job. Do you think ways of thinking matter? Use specific examples and explain.

搭配的暢銷書

- *Mistakes I Made at Work*《我工作中所犯的錯誤中》
- *The Job*《工作》

Step 1 ■ 題目是詢問關於在工作和生活中能取得平衡的工作。這題也不太好答，在缺乏許多實例時，是很難論述跟說服閱讀者。首段先由暢銷書《我工作中所犯的錯誤中》，金提到的看法，並進一步由另一本暢銷書《工作》的觀點，逐步導引出問題，「工作和生活中平衡的工作是否存在呢？」。

Step 2 ■ 次段提到在工作和生活中取得平衡的工作確實存在著，並提及這是夢幻工作，而找到夢幻工作還牽涉到其他條件，主要是表明有這樣的工作存在，但很稀少。

Step 3 ■ 下個段落提到，另一類型的工作，能提供求職者彈性工時的工作，這種類型的工作就能平衡工作跟家庭。

Step 4 ■ **末段提到思考模式，其實思考影響甚鉅**，很神奇的是，當你認為你能做到時，其實你就能做到，但當你覺得你只能擇一時，你人生終究只能擇一，而且你只能遠望別人兩者都擁有。

■（其實尤其像是在西方社會，有些女生當上高階主管，並同時養育了出色的小孩，同時享有家庭幸福跟職場成功，但也有當上高階主管但卻維持單身者，因為認為自己無法兼顧兩者，其實一開始的思維是否設限就影響蠻大，反而跟其他條件像是學經歷無關了。）

整合能力強化 ❹ 參考範文 ▶ *MP3 021*

經由先前的演練後，現在請看整篇範文並聆聽音檔

In *Mistakes I Made at Work*, Kim Gordon mentions **"The idea of "work-life balance" is not necessarily helpful. If you are immersed in your work and raising a family, you might feel a lot of good things – but it may not include balanced."** The statement seems to inform us that seeking a work-life balance job is so unlikely, and this is so discouraging. Another expert, a senior director at Goldman Sachs said **"the more you talk about work-life balance, the more you create the problem that you want to solve."** This further validates there is going to be an ensuing problem when you seek this kind of job. But does the job of work-life balance not exist?

在《我工作中所犯的錯誤中》，金・古登提到「工作－生活平衡的想法並不總是有助益」。如果你沉浸在你的工作和養育一個家庭，你可能會感覺到許多好事情 – 但是可能不會包含平衡」。這個陳述似乎是告知我們追求工作和生活平衡的工作是不可能的，而這是令人沮喪的。另一位專家，一位高勝資深經理說道「你越是談論到工作和生活平衡，你越是創造出你想要解決的問題」。這進一步地證實了，會有接踵而來的問題，當你找尋那樣的工作時。但是工作和生活中平衡的工作是否存在？

What experts have told us do have some valid and insightful points, but regardless of what experts tell us, the job of work-life balance does exist. It is the dream job, and it is not something that you seek. This puzzles many of us. But it is like what is described in the book, dream job is often created than found. Normally, it is not the job that you see on the job search pages. This could be the job for someone who has irreplaceable technical skills and job experiences, and recruiters deem you can be the one to do the job. But in the company, they do not have that kind of job title yet. The job is designed for someone who might have the skill to do things that can meet the future goals of the company. This kind of the job is exceptionally rare.

專家們已經告訴我們的確實是有些根據和洞察性的重點，但是不論專家們告訴我們什麼，工作和生活中取得平衡的工作確實存在著。這是夢幻工作，而非你追求而來的工作。這使我們大多數的人感到困惑。但這像是書中所述，夢幻工作通常是創造出來的，而非找到的。通常，這不是在你找工作的頁面中會看到的。但在公司中尚未有這個頭銜的工作存在。這可能是個替有些具有不可取代的專業技巧和工作經驗者所打造的，而招募者認為你是唯一一個可以做那個工作的人。這份工作是一些具有能力，可能能夠達到公司未來目標者所設計的。這樣的工作是相當罕見的。

In other occasions, it can be the work-life balance. Jobs that offer you to have a flexible work mode are the solution for the problem. Some jobs are flexible enough for you to work for certain days a week so that you can manage both your work and your family. Other jobs are jobs that can be done at home. These jobs are the cure for someone who has younger kids.

在其他時機，這可以是工作和生活的平衡。工作提供給你彈性的工作模式是這個問題的解決之道。有些工作讓你有足夠的彈性，每周的特定幾天你可以經營好你的工作和家庭。其他工作則是你能夠在家完成的。這些工作都是對於有較年輕的小孩者的治療之方。

Another thing about the work-life balance is that it is related to thinking patterns. You think you can manage both work and life, then you can do both. If you deem yourself as someone who can manage either work or life, then you can only manage either one. Thinking shapes how one performs. To sum up, I think with right thinking mindset, you can manage both life and work, even if you do not have the dream job. Our will is much powerful than what you think.

另一件關於工作和生活平衡的是關於思考模式。你認為你可能同時經營好工作和生活，那麼你就能做到。如果你認為你自己僅能處理好工作或生活其中之一，那麼你就僅能管理好其中一項。思考形塑一個人如何表現。總之，我認為有著對的思考模式，你可以管理好生活和工作，即使你沒有夢幻工作。我們的意志遠你比想像的要強大的多了。

UNIT 07

許多畢業生大學畢業後都有學貸，有些甚至需要在高中兼職打工。你認為學生該享受當下還是儘管家庭財務狀況許可，仍要打工呢？這對他們的未來有什麼影響呢？

Writing Task 2

TOPIC

There are multiple graduates, graduating from universities with lots of tuition debts and some even have to work part-time in high school. Others are lucky enough to have parents that tell them just enjoy their life for the moment and study. Do you think despite their upbringing and family's financial status, they should still find a part-time job? If so, what will that influence their future. Use specific examples and explain.

Write at least 250 words

整合能力強化 ❶ 實際演練

請搭配左頁的題目和並構思和完成大作文的演練。

整合能力強化 ❷ 單句中譯英演練

❶ 在《第一份工作》，創辦人 E.,分享了他的經驗，他的父母告訴他「有我生命的餘生去工作，而現在我應該僅僅需要學習和享受生活」。

____

____

【參考答案】

In *First Jobs*, a founder, E., shares his experience that his parents told him that he "had the rest of my life to work, and I should just study and enjoy life now."

❷ 我認為像是 E.這樣的人是非常幸運能有那樣子的父母，而且我並不反對寵小孩的這個想法。

____

____

【參考答案】

I think people like E., are very lucky to have that kind of parents, and I am not against the idea of pampering kids.

❸ 這某些程度上幫助我看到了現實世界中的另一瞥。

____

____

【參考答案】

It somehow helps me see another glimpse of the real world.

❹ 有些小孩在年紀很輕的階段就必須要開始工作了，但是我並沒有把他們視為是不幸運的類型。

____

____

【參考答案】

There are some kids who have to start to work at a very early age, but I do not view them as the unlucky type.

❺ 有些事情是你需要探索的，而在你大學四年的兼職工作就是其中一項。

____

____

【參考答案】

There are things that you need to explore, and working part time during four years of undergraduate study is one of them.

❻ 你能夠在學術環境之外做些什麼。你能夠在兼職工作之餘，學習如何處理問題。你在壓力之下能夠展示出你的工作能力。

____

____

【參考答案】

You can do something outside the academic environment. You can learn how to cope with problems during working part-time. You demonstrate your ability to work under pressure.

❼ 你最終可以了解到什麼類型的工作最適合你，而你不想要以什麼維生。你將會對於周遭的人和事情有全然不同的想法。

____

____

【參考答案】

You eventually figure what works best for you, and what you do not want to do for a living. You will have a totally different perspective to things and people around you.

❽ 或許你過去總認為錢很好賺，而藉由做些藍領工作，你了解到要賺一分錢有多麼艱難。

____

____

【參考答案】

Perhaps you used to think money is easily earned, and by doing some blue-collar jobs, you understand how hard it is to earn a cent.

❾ 你最終了解到你父母是多麼努力工作來支持你和你的家庭。

____

____

【參考答案】

You ultimately know how hard your parents have to work to support you and the family.

⑩ 這些事情都不是你在學校環境中可以學習的到的，而你必須要經由做去了解到，你正逐漸的轉變成一位感恩的人，而從做那樣的工作你了解到你未來的道路，你不想要從事哪些工作，例如藍領工作。

____

____

【參考答案】

This thing cannot be learned in the school setting, and you have to do it to realize that. you are gradually becoming a grateful person, and from doing that kind of job, you figure out your future path that you do not want to do jobs, such as blue-collar jobs.

TOPIC

There are multiple graduates, graduating from universities with lots of tuition debts and some even have to work part-time in high school. Others are lucky enough to have parents that tell them just enjoy their life for the moment and study. Do you think despite their upbringing and family's financial status, they should still find a part-time job? If so, what will that influence their future. Use specific examples and explain.

搭配的暢銷書

■ *First Job*s《第一份工作》

Step 1 ■ 題目是詢問是否要兼差打工呢，儘管經濟上不需要去打工，而打工對於一個人的影響又是什麼呢？先由《第一份工作》，創辦人 E 的經驗提到了與正常小孩都需要打工的不同的看法，而且提到並不反對寵小孩的看法。（父母其實對於小孩的養育方式是各式各樣的。）

Step 2 ■ 次段表達出「有些小孩在年紀很輕的階段就必須要開始工作了，但是我並沒有把他們視為是不幸運的類型。」，另外提到關於自我探索和必須在學術環境外，藉由兼職去了解自己想要什麼，不想要什麼，這點蠻重要的。

Step 3 ■ 再來提到藍領工作，從事這樣的兼職工作更能體會到父母的辛苦並且知道要感恩。

Step 4 ■ 最後提到心境的轉換，這是遠超乎自己想像的，尤其是對人處事。另一部分是，都沒有打工經驗，讓面試官對你產生質疑，而且在面試過程中沒有經驗可以分享，例如克服挫折等的體驗。有打工經驗者則較具吸引力。最後總結出，這跟家庭背景等是無關的，打工對於畢業生求職是有幫助的。

經由先前的演練後，現在請看整篇範文並聆聽音檔

In *First Jobs*, a founder, E., shares his experience that his parents told him that he "had the rest of my life to work, and I should just study and enjoy life now." I think people like E., are very lucky to have that kind of parents, and I am not against the idea of pampering kids. It somehow helps me see another glimpse of the real world.

在《第一份工作》，創辦人 E.,分享了他的經驗，他的父母告訴他「有我生命的餘生去工作，而現在我應該僅僅需要學習和享受生活」。我認為像是 E.這樣的人是非常幸運能有那樣子的父母，而且我並不反對寵小孩的這個想法。這某些程度上幫助我看到了現實世界中的另一瞥。

There are some kids who have to start to work at a very early age, but I do not view them as the unlucky type. There are things that you need to explore, and working part time during four years of undergraduate study is one of them. You can do something outside the academic environment. You can learn how to cope with problems during working part-time. You demonstrate your ability to work under pressure. You eventually figure what works best for you, and what you do not want to do for a living. You will have a totally different perspective to things and people around you.

有些小孩在年紀很輕的階段就必須要開始工作了，但是我並沒有把他們視為是不幸運的類型。有些事情是你需要探索的，而在你大學四年的兼職工作就是其中一項。你能夠在學術環境之外做些什麼。你能夠在兼職工作之餘，學習如何處理問題。你在壓力之下能夠展示出你的工作能力。你最終可以了解到什麼類型的工作最適合你，而你不想要以什麼維生。你將會對於周遭的人和事情有全然不同的想法。

Perhaps you used to think money is easily earned, and by doing some blue-collar jobs, you understand how hard it is to earn a cent. You ultimately know how hard your parents have to work to support you and the family. This thing cannot be learned in the school setting, and you have to do it to realize that. You are gradually becoming a grateful person, and from doing that kind of job, you figure out your future path that you do not want to do jobs, such as blue-collar jobs.

或許你過去總認為錢很好賺，而藉由做些藍領工作，你了解到要賺一分錢有多麼艱難。你最終了解到你父母是多麼努力工作來支持你和你的家庭。這些事情都不是你在學校環境中可以學習的到的，而你必須要經由做去了解到，你正逐漸的轉變成一位感恩的人，而從做那樣的工作你了解到你未來的道路，你不想要從事哪些工作，例如藍領工作。

The mind-shifting makes you a changed person. When you are back to school, you have become a more focused person. You really want to perfect your skills so that you will get an ideal white-collar job after you graduate. The repercussions are more than what you can think of. You treat things differently. All these cannot be done if you have not done any part-time job, and it is actually a plus when you are looking for a job. It can be a story for you to share whether it is something that you do not do well, but eventually learn how to do it well. Interviewers will take that kind of things to heart, but when you solely focus on the study and without these experiences, you have nothing to say during the job search. It really makes you less intriguing.

心境的轉換讓你成了個全然不同的人。當你回到學校之後，你已經成了一位更具專注的人。你真的想要完善你的技能，這樣一來你就能夠在你畢業後有理想的白領工作。這些影響是超乎你想像的。你對待事情的方式也不同了。如果你沒有做過任何兼職工作，所有這些都無法達成，實際上這對於你要找工作也是加分的。這可以成為你所能分享的故事，不論是一些你沒做好的事情，但是最終學習如何把它做好。面試官們會把這些聽進心頭裡，但當你僅專注於學習上，而沒有這些經驗時，你在找工作時就沒有東西可以分享。這讓你看起來較不具吸引力。

To sum up, I think it has nothing to do with the family's financial status and backgrounds. Doing a few part-time jobs helps graduates in the long term.

總之，我認為這與一個家庭的財務狀況和背景無關。長遠來說，從事幾份兼職工作對畢業生是有幫助的。

UNIT 08 父母教育小孩的方式影響孩子成長和自我探索。孩子會隱藏起他們的情感，但父母又必須和小孩建立起適當的連結。怎麼拿捏會比較好。

TOPIC

Parents in different districts or various nations will tend to favor a certain approach to raise and educate their kids. Some prefer to spend most of the time taking their kids traveling, exercising in the park, or visiting museums so that their children can develop their own interest along the way. Others are inclined to set a strict rule for their own kids, learning things solely related to school tests or the college entrance exam. What is your opinion on this topic?

Write at least 250 words

整合能力強化 ❶ 實際演練

請搭配左頁的題目和並構思和完成大作文的演練。

整合能力強化 ❷ 單句中譯英演練

❶ 最佳的時間利用是否該花在玩遊戲或運動上或是家庭作業上，一直以來一直是備受爭論的，但是主要的焦點應該要設定在了解你的孩子。

____

____

【參考答案】
Whether the best use of the time should be spent on playing games or sports or homework has long been debated, but the main focus should be set on understanding your kids.

❷ 即使有著每週聚集在晚餐餐桌的集會，小孩能夠隱藏他們的情感，在表面上僅分享出在學校中所發生的正面的事物。

____

____

【參考答案】
Even if there is a weekly gathering at the dinner table, kids can hide their emotions, and on the surface only sharing all the positive things happening in the school.

❸ 父母所能做的就是將有限的時間花費在與小孩子玩遊戲或運動上，尤其是這是他們感到放鬆的時候，但是若是將時間花費在學校作業上可能僅有著壞的成果，導致更多的家庭紛爭。

【參考答案】

What parents can do is spend their limited time playing games or sports with them, especially it is the time they feel relaxed, but spending time doing schoolwork with them can bring only bad outcomes, resulting in more family feuds.

❹ 他們不會說些傷人的話，而且同班同學有時候在相同的處境上，仍在試圖了解著有些數學問題或正開始準備 SAT 測驗，而父母因為自己已經有了這些體驗了，會超越小孩的表現。

【參考答案】

They won't say something hurtful, and classmates are sometimes at the same situation, still figuring some math problems or starting to prepare SAT, whereas parents outperform their kids because they had done those things before.

❺ 既然父母不是學校作業時間的良好候選人，他們取而代之的是，應該與小孩子玩遊戲或從事運動活動。

【參考答案】

Since parents are not good candidates for the schoolwork time, they should instead play games or sports with kids.

❻ 這是他們能夠了解孩子的時候，像是小孩是如何思考玩足球的策略和為什麼他們會這樣思考或是他們如何與兄弟姊妹、朋友、家庭成員合作或是小孩是個良好的團隊合作者嗎？

【參考答案】

It is the time they can understand their kids, like how kids think about the strategy of playing football and why they think that way or how they cooperate with siblings, friends, family members, or are kids a good team player?

❼ 所有這些父母在學校作業無法察覺的事情能發揮效用，這比起我的小孩在數學表現多好或是我的小孩在拼字比賽上表現多好更重要。

【參考答案】

All these things that parents won't find during school time work, and it is something more important than how well my kids do in math or how well my kids perform at the spelling bees.

❽ 其中之一的主婦，麗奈特・思嘉夫在第一季時有四個小孩。有次他對著警察宣洩著自己的情緒「我有四個年紀六歲以下的小孩要養育。我當然會有情緒控管問題。」，但是她卻也展示出一些與這主題相關的部分。

【參考答案】

One time she vented her emotions to the policeman that "I have four kids under the age of six. I absolutely have anger management issue", but she also demonstrates something related to the topic.

❾ 藉由與她的小孩玩棒球，她展現出她的耐心，即使她笑著說：如果我把棒球在丟慢些，那就是在打保齡球了。

【參考答案】

By playing baseball with her kid, she shows her patience even though she laughs like if I threw a little slower, then it would be playing bowling.

❿ 小孩在乎的是當他們本身正對於學習某些事情感到掙扎時，他們的父母是否能夠對他們表現出耐心，但大多數的父母卻不是這麼做，將小孩推的離他們更遠了。

【參考答案】

Kids care about whether their parents can show patience to them when they are obviously struggling to learn things, and most of the time parents are doing the opposite pushing their kids further away from them.

整合能力強化 ❸ 段落拓展

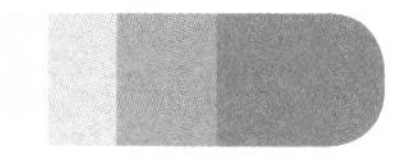

TOPIC

Parents in different districts or various nations will tend to favor a certain approach to raise and educate their kids. Some prefer to spend most of the time taking their kids traveling, exercising in the park, or visiting museums so that their children can develop their own interest along the way. Others are inclined to set a strict rule for their own kids, learning things solely related to school tests or the college entrance exam. What is your opinion on this topic?

搭配的暢銷書

■ Desperate Housewives《慾望師奶》

Step 1 ■ 父母會選擇教育孩子的方式很多，看完題目後可以先思考下要如何構思這篇文章，題目中提到的兩個方向是不同的，一個偏向讓小孩經由去博物館等探索自我，而另一種則偏向傳統型教育模式。

Step 2 ■ 範文的開頭是先點出要先了解孩子，才能逐步思考出到底什麼方式會更適合孩子，接著指出「主要的焦點應該要設定在了解你的孩子」並進一步闡述。

Step 3 ■ **用對比的方式陳述出「父母」扮演的角色和「教師、同班同學、親密朋友和指導員」之間的不同**，並說明父母若把時間花在遊戲和運動上，則家庭更和樂。（父母的體驗或考試經驗已經先入為主的影響孩子學習，但孩子並非父母本身，且每個人學習情況不同，反推回去會造成親子關係不佳。）

Step 4 ■ **次個段落繼續針對前個段落中的重點進一步說明**，首句就引入主題「既然父母不是學校作業時間的良好候選人，他們取而代之的是，應該與小孩子玩遊戲或從事運動活動。」。緊接著接續提問，讓讀者反思。於接續的問句後再次講述與孩子遊戲或運動的優點，且這遠比分數重要多了。

Step 5 ■ 最後的段落提到《慾望師奶》中小孩教養的部分和智慧，除了能引起考官或讀者共鳴外，也能提升說服力，並由當中教育孩子的部分，進一步強化立場達到說服效果。生動的表明出劇中教育孩子的部分也是加分點，能與坊間範文或其他考生的回答作出區隔，一舉獲取高分。

Whichever the approach parents will choose, the main focus should be set on "Really Understanding You Kids". Understanding kids can be quite hard simply because kids don't always tell you everything. Even if there is a weekly gathering at the dinner table, kids can hide their emotions, and on the surface only sharing all the positive things happening in the school.

不論父母會選擇哪個方法，主要的重點應該要設定在「了解你的孩子。」因為孩子不會總是告訴你每件事，所以了解孩子可能相當困難。即使有著每週聚集在晚餐餐桌的集會，孩子會隱藏起他們的情感，在表面上僅分享出在學校中所發生的正面的事物。

What parents can do is spend their limited time playing games or sports with them, especially it is the time kids feel relaxed, but spending time doing schoolwork with them can bring only bad outcomes, resulting in more family feuds. Teachers, classmates, close friends, and tutors can be the better person than parents to do the schoolwork time. They won't say something hurtful, and classmates are sometimes at the same situation, still figuring some math problems or starting to prepare SAT, whereas parents outperform their kids because they had done those things before.

父母所能做的就是將有限的時間花費在與小孩子玩遊戲或運動上，尤其是這是孩子們感到放鬆的時候，但是若是僅將時間花費在學校作業上可能有壞的成果，導致更多的家庭紛爭。比起父母，教師、同班同學、親密朋友和指導員在學習上能扮演著更好的角色。他們不會說些傷人的話，而且同班同學有時候處於相同的處境上，仍在試圖了解有些數學問題或正開始準備 SAT 測驗，而父母因為自己已經有了這些體驗了，會超越小孩的表現。

Since parents are not good candidates for the schoolwork time, they should instead play games or sports with kids. It is the time they can understand their kids, like how kids think about the strategy of playing football and why they think that way or how they cooperate with siblings, friends, family members, or are kids a good team player? Or how kids crack the puzzle? All these things that parents won't find during school time work, and it is something more important than how well my kids do in math or how well my kids perform at the spelling bees. It is something that will shape his character and personality. It is something that builds the bond between parents and kids.

既然父母不是學校作業時間的稱職候選人，取而代之的是，他們應該與小孩子玩遊戲或從事運動活動。這是他們能夠了解孩子的時候，像是小孩是如何思考玩足球的策略和為什麼他們會這樣思考或是他們如何與兄弟姊妹、朋友、家庭成員合作或是小孩是個良好的團隊合作者嗎？或是小孩是如何解開謎團的呢？所有這些父母在學校作業無法察覺的事情能發揮效用，這比起我的小孩在數學表現上或是我的小孩在拼字比賽上表現得有多好更為重要。這是形塑他們角色和個性的時候。這也是父母和小孩們建立情感連結的時候。

In one of the successful sitcoms, *Desperate Housewives*, it uncovers some wisdom of how parents raise kids or how four housewives raise kids. It is something audiences can learn from. One of the housewives, Lynette Scavo has four kids in season one. One time she vented her emotions to the policeman that "I have four kids under the age of six. I absolutely have anger management issue", but she also demonstrates something related to the topic. She does spend time with kids by playing sports even if her husband says their kids are not the baseball material so he doesn't have to play. By playing baseball with her kid, she shows her patience even though she laughs like **"if I threw a little slower, then it would be playing bowling."** She wants her kid to have the personality to not quit doing things, and most important of all she understands her kid. Kids need that kind of support. Kids care about whether their parents can show patience to them when they are obviously struggling to learn things, and most of the time parents are doing the opposite pushing their kids further away from them. So from above-mentioned reasons, I prefer to let kids do several activities so that they can explore themselves and can find their own interest.

在其中一部成功的情境喜劇《慾望師奶》中，它揭露了一些父母如何養育小孩或是四個主婦如何養育小孩的智慧。這是一些觀眾們能夠學習的部分。其中之一的主婦，麗奈特 思嘉夫在第一季時有四個小孩。有次他對著警察宣洩著自己的情緒「我有四個年紀六歲以下的小孩要養育。我當然會有情緒控管問題。」，但是她卻也展示出一些與這主題相關的部分。她花費時間與小孩們從事運動活動，即使她丈夫表明了他們小孩不是打棒球的料，所以他不需要練棒球。藉由與她的小孩玩棒球，她展現出她的耐心，即使她笑著說：「如果我把棒球在丟慢些，那就是在打保齡球了。」她想要自己的小孩能夠有著不放棄做任何事的個性，而最重要的是她了解她的小孩。小孩需要那樣的情感支持。小孩在乎的是當他們本身正對於學習某些事情感到掙扎時，他們的父母是否能夠對他們表現出耐心，但大多數的父母卻不是這麼做，將小孩推的離他們更遠了。所以從上述的這些理由，我偏好讓小孩做幾項活動，這樣一來他們能夠探索自我和找到他們自己的興趣。

UNIT 09 父母教育影響小孩作決定和獨立，過多的保護反而有害。對此你有什麼看法，請以具體實例去解釋。

Writing Task 2

TOPIC

Decision making is quite essential in our life, but nowadays parents tend to be the ones responsible for kids' inability to make major decisions and be independent. People from the previous generation; however, had no troubles making a major decision. What do you think about these statements?

Write at least 250 words

整合能力強化 ❶ 實際演練

請搭配左頁的題目和並構思和完成大作文的演練。

整合能力強化 ❷ 單句中譯英演練

❶ 校園環境是衡量學生使否有能力自力和能夠對於他們自己本身生活做出重大決定的指標之一。

【參考答案】

Campus settings are one of the indicators to measure whether or not students are able to stand on their own feet and are able to make major decisions for their own life.

❷ 不同於在《你如何衡量你的人生》一書中所描述的足球父母們，會替他們的小孩安排太多事情，現今的父母們對於自己的小孩則太過於保護。他們不斷地擔憂著小孩。

【參考答案】

Unlike what is described in *How Will You Measure Your Life*, the soccer parents, who arranged too many things for their kids, today's parents are too protective of their kids. They are constantly worried about them.

❸ 在學校裡，父母不是從遠距離的地方拜訪他們的小孩，卻是從事著替小孩們清掃的工作。

【參考答案】
In campus, parents are not visiting their kids from a far distance but doing the cleaning for their kids.

❹ 有位學校校長回憶，接道數通來自父母的電話，關於學校政策不適合他們的孩子。

【參考答案】
One headmaster recalled getting calls from parents about school policies not quite suitable for their kids.

❺ 或是教授接到父母的電話，告知他們的小孩需要請假。

【參考答案】
Or professors getting calls from parents that their kids want to take a leave of absence.

❽ 年輕人替自己做決定的能力不是稍微退步些，而是有大幅步的退步，根據許多教授的陳述。

____

____

【參考答案】

Young people's ability to make decisions is not just regressing for a bit, but quite a lot, according to many professors.

❼ 你如何能期待孩子做重大的決定，當孩子們連像是向教授請假的這些微不足道的小事都需要父母代勞呢？

____

____

【參考答案】

How can you expect kids to make major decisions about life when they cannot make something as trivial as asking for a leave of absence to professors in person.

❽ 其他教授甚至接到來自父母的來電，告知他們既然這是知名的大學，在競爭上會異常激烈，他們不希望看到他們的小孩的自尊受到傷害。

____

____

【參考答案】
Other professors even getting calls from parents informing them that since it's a well-known university, competition is so fierce that they don't want to see their kids' feelings getting hurt.

❾ 年輕人卻束手無策因為他們已經適應了，從母親子宮出生後，父母都會替他們打算的日子了。

____

____

【參考答案】
Young people can do nothing about it simply because they have accustomed to what their parents will do for them right after they come out of mother's womb.

❿ 這已經成了習慣，父母們會做像是替他們打掃這樣子微不足道的小事到替他們撰寫履歷和打電話給公司的人事專員。

____

____

【參考答案】
It has become a habit that their parents will do things as trivial as cleaning to something as major as writing a resume and making a phone call to the company's HR personnel.

整合能力強化 ❸ 段落拓展

TOPIC

Decision making is quite essential in our life, but nowadays parents tend to be the ones responsible for kids' inability to make major decisions and be independent. People from the previous generation; however, had no troubles making a major decision. What do you think about these statements?

搭配的暢銷書

■ *How Will You Measure Your Life*《你如何衡量你的人生》

Step 1 ■ 看完題目後先寫出概述句，定義出「在校園環境是衡量學生使否有能力自力和能夠對於他們自己本身生活做出重大決定的指標之一。」，這段於後面要寫出題目中提到的「孩子更難獨立跟做決定等」是相關聯的，也更好去延伸段落。

Step 2 ■ 選擇好立場後，列出陳述句後緊接著表明事情並非如此，並使用《你如何衡量你的人生》一書中所描述的足球父母們，強化不同意的立場，過度替小孩安排事情的足球父母，造成了小孩子過於依賴等問題，除了呼應首句，也會下個段落作了鋪陳。

Step 3 ■ **舉出實例**，包含校長和教授接到電話的部分，還有使用誇飾「根據許多教授的陳述，年輕人替自己做決定的能力不是稍微退步些，而是有大幅步地退步。」還有反問等接續對不同意這個論點進行論述，清楚點出不同意的原因。這些都導致了年輕人無法替自己的人生做出重大的決定。

Step 4 ■ 有了暢銷書加持後，就要利用當中的論點協助表達出接續的文句，文中提到了困惑處和該父親堅持不給予小孩金錢的等值獎勵，此能大幅強化我們不支持提供獎勵的論點。

Step 5 ■ 最後一段更詼諧地描述「年輕人卻束手無策因為他們已經適應了，從母親子宮出生後，父母都會替他們打算的日子了。」。「這已經成了習慣，父母們會做像是替他們打掃這樣子微不足道的小事到替他們撰寫履歷和打電話給公司的人事專員。」最後以因為這些因素所以不同意題目論述作為結束。

整合能力強化 ❹ 參考範文 ▶ MP3 024

Campus settings are one of the indicators to measure whether or not students are able to stand on their own feet and are able to make major decisions for their own life. Recently, what has been observed by reporters, professors, and school headmasters shows this has never been the case. Students are too reliant on their parents to make decisions for them. Unlike what is described in *How Will You Measure Your Life*, the soccer parents, who arranged too many things for their kids, today's parents are too protective of their kids. They are constantly worried about them.

校園環境是衡量學生使否有能力自力和能夠對於他們自己本身生活做出重大決定的指標之一。最近，記者們、教授們和學校校長們表示，事情卻不是如此。學生太依賴父母來替他們做出決定。不同於在《你如何衡量你的人生》一書中所描述的足球父母們，會替他們的小孩安排太多事情，現今的父母們對於自己的小孩則太過於保護。他們不斷地擔憂著小孩。

In campus, parents are not visiting their kids from a far distance but doing the cleaning for their kids. One headmaster recalled getting calls from parents about school policies not quite suitable for their kids. Or professors getting calls from parents that their kids want to take a leave of absence. Something is going wrong in the campus.

Young people's ability to make decisions is not just regressing for a bit, but quite a lot, according to many professors. How can you expect kids to make major decisions about life when they cannot make something as trivial as asking for a leave of absence to professors in person.

在學校裡，父母不是從遠距離的地方拜訪他們的小孩，卻是從事著替小孩們清掃的工作。有位學校校長回憶，接到數通來自父母的電話，關於學校政策不適合他們的孩子。或是教授接到父母的電話，告知他們的小孩需要請假。在校園中出現這些事情顯然這些不太對勁。年輕人替自己做決定的能力不是稍微退步，而是有大幅地退步，根據許多教授的陳述。當孩子們連像是向教授請假的這些微不足道的小事都需要父母代勞，你如何能期待孩子做重大的決定呢？

Other professors even getting calls from parents informing them that since it's a well-known university, competition is so fierce that they don't want to see their kids' feelings getting hurt. Parents' interference and over protection is one of the reasons harming today's young people, resulting in not being able to make decisions for their own life.

其他教授甚至接到來自父母的來電，告知他們既然這是知名的大學，在競爭上會異常激烈，他們不希望看到他們的小孩的自尊受到傷害。父母的干預和過度的保護是傷害現今年輕人的主因之一，導致年輕人無法替自己的人生做出重大的決定。

Today's young people are like roses in the greenhouse, compared with young people in the past. Young people can do nothing about it simply because they have accustomed to what their parents will do for them right after they come out of mother's womb. It has become a habit that their parents will do things as trivial as cleaning to something as major as writing a resume and making a phone call to the company's HR personnel. Some parents are even going to the interview with their kids and doing all the talking. All these make interviewers not convince candidates' ability to do the job. From all these reasons, perhaps today's parents should dial back to how parents raised kids from the previous generations so that kids can develop a sound mindset and decision-making ability. Therefore, I think these statements are so true.

跟過去的年輕人相比，現今的年輕人就像是溫室的玫瑰般。年輕人卻束手無策因為他們已經適應了，從母親子宮出生後，父母都會替他們打算的日子了。這已經成了習慣，父母們會做像是替他們打掃這樣子微不足道的小事到替他們撰寫履歷和打電話給公司的人事專員。有些父母甚至陪同小孩去參加面試，而且全程都替小孩子回答。這些都讓面試官們無法信服候選人有做這份工作的能力。從這些原因來看，或許今日的父母應該要將事情撥回正軌，撥回至上一代父母如何養育小孩，這樣他們的小孩才能夠發展出健全的心態且具備做決定的能力。因此，我認為這些陳述是很真實的。

UNIT 10 主修科系的選擇和未來前途：儘管關於選系的傳統觀點有些有事實理據，但職涯軌跡並不是能預測的。人們無法很確定選擇某個特定的科系就意謂著未來會更成功。

Writing Task 2

TOPIC

Traditional viewpoints have often favored students majoring in engineering and hard science over students of the humanities and social sciences, thinking that the latter has a less promising future right after students graduate from universities. Thus, people are suggesting that we should not major in History or Philosophy. What is your opinion?

Write at least 250 words

整合能力強化 ❶ 實際演練

請搭配左頁的題目和並構思和完成大作文的演練。

整合能力強化 ❷ 單句中譯英演練

❶ 歷史無疑是每個國家的基礎，且其重要性是不能被低估的。

【參考答案】

Without a doubt, history is the foundation for every country, and its importance cannot be downgraded.

❷ 在現今的社會中，許多學科都受到低估，因為父母和教學家們想要他們的孩子和下一代，在步入就業市場時，學習對他們立即有效用的事物，但是我們的社會正經歷著急遽的改變，這種改變是如此地無法預測和難以想像的。

【參考答案】

In today's society, a lot of subjects are undervalued due to the fact that parents and educators want their kids and future generations to learn things that can have immediate effects when they enter the job market, but our society is undergoing a drastic change, a change that is so unpredictable and imaginable.

❸ 我們今日所認定有用的技能可能與幾年內就過時了，而且僅專注於從事特定的事情會在某些程度上危害到我們本身，而這也是我們料想未及的。

____

____

【參考答案】
Skills that we deem useful today can be outdated in a few years, and solely focusing on doing a certain thing can harm us in a way that we cannot imagine.

❹ 主修商業的學生將重心放在如何獲取商業相關的證照或是參加與商業相關的研討會，完全沒意識到這樣雖使得他們能夠找到工作，但長遠來說對他們來說卻不是最好的。

____

____

【參考答案】
Students majoring in commerce will solely focus on getting the certificate related to commerce or attending seminars relevant to business, totally forgetting the fact that doing this only makes them able to find the job, but will not do them good in the long-term.

❺ 這是她所寫道的「許多學生太專注於獲取對的分數，這樣他們才能夠進入對的學校，但如此卻使得他們無法從事些不尋常的事」。

【參考答案】

This is what she wrote "Many students are so focused on getting the right grades so that they can get into the right school that it barely gives them the chance to do something zany".

❻ 她最終修習俄羅斯歷史。修俄羅斯歷史不僅使她更了解自己，也替她未來的成功鋪路。

【參考答案】

She eventually took Russian history. Taking Russian history not only makes her more realize herself, but also paves the path for her future success.

❼ 她創造出幾部電影都是大熱門，因為她熟悉歷史人物。

【參考答案】

She created several movies that were great hits due to the fact that she knew historical figures.

❽ 她的經驗告訴我們，我們不可能真的預測出什麼對我們來說是最有利的而且修習歷史課碰巧在她工作中扮演了關鍵的角色。

【參考答案】
Her experience tells us that we cannot really predict what will benefit us and taking history classes happens to play the key role in her job.

9. 每個主要事件的發生或歷史人物所做的主要決定形塑著我們的思考，而且在我們有困難時給予我們所需要的智慧。

【參考答案】
Every major events happening or major decisions made by historical figures shapes our thinking and gives us wisdom we need at the time of the need.

10. 有時候那些事情幫助我們思考著有些超越當今思考的事情，使我們配著更棒的創造力和解決之道，對於那些尚未全然理解出頭緒的事物有更好的處理方式。

【參考答案】
Sometimes those things help us think about something that transcend current thinking, packaging us with greater creativity and solutions for things not yet fully understood.

整合能力強化 ❸ 段落拓展

TOPIC

Traditional viewpoints have often favored students majoring in engineering and hard science over students of the humanities and social sciences, thinking that the latter has a less promising future right after students graduate from universities. Thus, people are suggesting that we should not major in History or Philosophy. What is your opinion?

搭配的暢銷書

- *Getting There*《勝利，並非事事順利：30 位典範人物不藏私的人生真心話》

Step 1

- 先思考主修人文社會科學和理工科系的優缺點。主修人文社會科學像是歷史和哲學真的是錯誤的選擇嗎？

Step 2 範文首句提供了很好的定義：

- 儘管關於選系的傳統觀點有些有事實理據，職涯軌跡並不是能預測的。
- 人們無法很確定的表明主修某個特定的科系就意謂著你一定會比主修其他科系更成功。

■ 因此我想使用歷史作為例子，講述主修人文和社會科學也能給予你特定的優勢。

（三句話很系統且邏輯性的引入主題。）

Step 3 ■ 藉由歷史為例子，除講到優勢外，也點出因為「父母和教育家們想要他們的孩子和下一代，在步入就業市場時，學習對他們立即有效用的事物」，這根深蒂固的思考，對於孩子在選擇主修造成了影響。

Step 4 ■ 提到暢銷書 Getting There，以史黛西・史奈德為例子，揭露了如何免於落入該圈套和如何從研讀俄羅斯歷史最終使她功成名就的智慧。

■「許多學生太專注於獲取對的分數，這樣他們才能夠進入對的學校，但如此卻使得他們無法從事些不尋常的事」。她最終修習俄羅斯歷史。修俄羅斯歷史不僅使她更了解自己，也替她未來的成功鋪路。

（這些都強化了文章的論點，提到人文社會科學的優勢，並解釋道我們不可能預測的到，學習哪些事物對自己本身是最有益處的。）

Step 5 ■ 最後解釋學習歷史的好處，並總結出「我們不該受到傳統觀點而有所侷限。放寬心胸去學習所有事物，對於面對未來才是最充分的準備。

整合能力強化 ❹ 參考範文 ▶ *MP3 025*

Although conventional viewpoints about choosing majors have some valid facts, career trajectory cannot be predicted. People cannot be certain that having a specific major means you are bound to be successful than the others. Thus, I would love to use history as an example to illustrate that majoring in humanities and social sciences can still give you certain advantages.

儘管關於選系的傳統觀點有些有事實理據，職涯軌跡並不是能預測的。人們無法很確定的表明主修某個特定的科系就意謂著你一定會比主修其他科系更成功。因此我想使用歷史作為例子，講述主修人文和社會科學也能給予你特定的優勢。

Without a doubt, history is the foundation for every country, and its importance cannot be downgraded. In today's society, a lot of subjects are undervalued due to the fact that parents and educators want their kids and future generations to learn things that can have immediate effects when they enter the job market, but our society is undergoing a drastic change, a change that is so unpredictable and imaginable. Skills that we deem useful today can be outdated in a few years, and solely focusing on doing a certain thing can harm us in a way that we cannot imagine.

歷史無疑是每個國家的基礎，且其重要性是不能被低估的。在現今的社會中，許多學科都受到低估，因為父母和教學家們想要他們的孩子和下一代，在步入就業市場時，學習對他們立即有效的事物，但是我們的社會正經歷著急遽的改變，這種改變是如此地無法預測和難以想像的。我們今日所認定有用的技能可能在幾年內就過時了，而且僅專注於從事特定的事情會在某些程度上危害到我們本身，而這也是我們料想未及的。

University students are now falling into that trap. Students majoring in commerce will solely focus on getting the certificate related to commerce or attending seminars relevant to business, totally forgetting the fact that doing this only makes them able to find the job, but will not do them good in the long-term.

大學學生正落入這樣的圈套。主修商業的學生將重心放在如何獲取商業相關的證照或是參加與商業相關的研討會，完全沒意識到這樣雖使得他們能夠找到工作，但長遠來說對他們來說卻不是最好的。

In "*Getting There*", one of the mentors, Stacey Snider reveals the wisdom of how to avoid the trap and how studying Russian history eventually makes how she is today. This is what she wrote "Many students are so focused on getting the right grades so that they can get into the right school that it barely gives them the chance to do something zany". She eventually took Russian history. Taking Russian history not only makes her more realize herself, but also paves the path for her future success. (She created several movies that were great hits due to the fact that she knew historical figures.) Her experience tells us that we cannot really predict what will benefit us and taking history classes happens to play the key role in her job. As can be seen in the case of Steve Jobs, Steve Jobs does not know how handwriting will help him design iPhone.

在「勝利，並非事事順利：30 位典範人物不藏私的人生真心話」一書中，史黛西 史奈德揭露了如何免於落入該圈套和研讀俄羅斯歷史如何使她最終功成名就的智慧。這是她所寫道的「許多學生太專注於獲取對的分數，這樣他們才能夠進入對的學校，但如此卻使得他們無法從事些不尋常的事」。她最終修習俄羅斯歷史。修俄羅斯歷史不僅使她更了解自己，也替她未來的成功鋪路。（她創造出幾部電影都是大熱門，因為她熟悉歷史人物。）她的經驗告訴我們，我們不可能真的預測出什麼對我們來說是最有利的，而且修習歷史課碰巧在她工作中扮演了關鍵的角色。像是賈伯斯那樣，當初也不知道手寫字對於設計 iPhone 有助益。

Apart from avoiding the limitation we set on ourselves, history transcends time and place. It even crosses multiple generations. It includes two major functions: wisdom and humanity. Historical figures make us realize the wisdom from a certain person and the mind of different people. Every major events happening or major decisions made by historical figures shapes our thinking and gives us wisdom we need at the time of the need. Sometimes those things help us think about something that transcend current thinking, packaging us with greater creativity and solutions for things not yet fully understood. Sometimes it is about people. Learning personality from different historical figures smooths the frictions among people and makes us succeed, so from the above-mentioned reasons, I do think all high school graduates or university students should not be restricted to conventional views. They should be open to all fields of studies so that they can be fully prepared than those who do not.

除了能避免對於我們自我設限之外，歷史超越時間和地點。它甚至跨越數個世代。它包含了兩個主要功能：智慧和人性。歷史人物使得我們了解到某些特定的人的智慧和不同人的心智。每個主要事件的發生或歷史人物所做的主要決定形塑著我們的思考，而且在我們有困難時給予我們所需要的智慧。有時候那些事情幫助我們思考著有些能超越當今思考的事情，使我們配著更棒的創造力和解決之道，對於那些尚未全然理解出頭緒的事物有更好的處理方式。有時候是關於人。學習不同的歷史人物的個性磨合人們間的摩擦和使我們成功，所以從上述的理由，我認為所有高中畢業生和大學學生都不該受到傳統觀點而有所侷限。他們應該對所有領域的研究都展開心胸看待，這樣他們才能比起那些不能敞開心胸的人有更充分的準備。

UNIT 11 孩童學習以及父母替孩子安排過多的活動，過與不及其實都不好。

Writing Task 2

TOPIC

Today's parents arrange an endless array of activities for their kids, leaving them too occupied to rest and cannot truly engage in something they are passionate about. Kids do need time to absorb those things and learning should not be forced and arranged. It should be based on children's interest. What is your opinion?

Write at least 250 words

整合能力強化 ❶ 實際演練

請搭配左頁的題目和並構思和完成大作文的演練。

整合能力強化 ❷ 單句中譯英演練

❶ 父母有著所有好的意圖，想要他們的孩子在起步上領先，但是這揭露了令人擔憂的部分。

____

____

【參考答案】

Parents all have good intentions of wanting their kids to start ahead, but it also uncovers something worrisome.

❷ 在「你如何衡量你的人生」一書中，讓你的孩子航行在賽修斯的船上揭露了擔憂，這能將我們導向去思考著主題，是否該給予小孩更多時間從事自己想做的事情。

____

____

【參考答案】

In "*How will you Measure Your Life*", the chapter of sailing your kids on Theseus's ship reveals worries that might direct us to think about the topic of whether kids should be given more time to do whatever they want.

❸ 相當值得嘉許的是活動能給予小孩更多的機會去自我探索，但是也可能是作者所描述的「父母，通常有著心之所向，將自己本身的希望和夢想投射在自己的小孩上面」或是「當這些其他意圖不知不覺的開始作用時，父母似乎將他們的小孩導向無止盡的活動列表上，但這卻非小孩子真的有意願從事的...」。

【參考答案】

It's quite commendable to give children lots of opportunities to explore themselves, but it can be what the author describes "parents, often with their heart in the right place, project their own hopes and dreams onto their children" or "when these other intentions start creeping in, and parents seem to be charting their children around to an endless array of activities in which the kids are not truly engaged…".

❹ 父母的投射或教師的期望可能在某種程度上傷害著小孩，讓小孩誤以為這些事情是他們應該要做的，但是數年後或是在小孩完成了某個學位後，小孩們發現自己在尷尬的處境上。

【參考答案】

Parents' projection or teachers' expectations can harm kids in a certain way, letting kids falsely believe it is something they should do, but years later or after kids have accomplished the degree, they find themselves in an awkward position.

❺ 精通法律的小孩想要學習商業知識。

【參考答案】

Kids specialized in law want to learn business knowledge.

❻ 此外，如果這不是小孩感到熱情的或是實際想從事的，這可能全然浪費時間和金錢。

【參考答案】

In addition, if it is not something kids are passionate about or truly engaged, it can be a total waste of time and money.

❼ 安排活動應該要基於小孩的興趣，如此才能將學習的力量最大化並且有助益於往後的成功。

【參考答案】

Arranged activities should be based on kids' interest so that it can maximize the power of learning and benefits for later success.

❽ 回到主題上，應該給予小孩更多時間從事他們所想要做的事，因為學習不該是經由安排的。

____

____

【參考答案】

Back to the topic, children should be given more time to do whatever they want because learning should not be arranged.

❾ 小孩應該要在閒暇時，發展出自己的興趣，不論是在海洋博物館的家庭旅遊中，想要知道更多有關於海洋生活。

____

____

【參考答案】

Kids should develop their own interest during leisure time whether it is about wanting to know more about marine life during the family trips in marine museums.

❿ 學習應該是要自動自發的，而非強迫的。

____

____

【參考答案】

Learning should be spontaneous, and it should not be forced.

TOPIC

Today's parents arrange an endless array of activities for their kids, leaving them too occupied to rest and cannot truly engage in something they are passionate about. Kids do need time to absorb those things and learning should not be forced and arranged. It should be based on children's interest. What is your opinion?

搭配的暢銷書

■ *How Will You Measure Your Life*《你如何衡量你的人生》

Step 1 ■ 這題是關於子女教育的問題，題目中的敘述中呈現了某一個論點，並詢問考生看法為何？若想表達的論點跟題目同，可以延續題目中提到的論點並接續表達看法，如果有其他不同於題目敘述的想法，可以思考下替小孩安排許多活動更多的優點等。

Step 2 首段除了先定義出「活動和這些意圖對小孩的影響」，接著使用暢銷書「你如何衡量你的人生」中的兩個具體的舉例：

■ **「父母，通常有著心之所向，將自己本身的希望和夢想投射在自己的小孩上面」。**

■ **「當這些其他意圖不知不覺的開始作用時，父母似乎將他們的小孩導向無止盡的活動列表上，但這卻非小孩子真的有意願從事的...」。**

■ 這兩句都闡述了父母對小孩造成了影響，並且留了許多可以討論的空間，這些影響都使得我們去思考題目所說的「安排活動」，這是父母加在小孩身上的，下段可以再藉由這部分的重點作進一步的論述。

Step 3 ■ 這段延續講述父母的投射和教師的期望，並指出如果這些活動和過程中儘管學習的項目頗多，但是若非小孩子本身感到熱情或想從事的，最終對小孩子並不是最好的。

Step 4 ■ 緊接著拉回主題上，應該讓小孩作自我探索並找到興趣，並指出「學習應該是要逐步發展的而且是由內部驅策的。」

Step 5 ■ 最後呼應題目敘述，講述大腦確實需要時間去吸收新知，孩子才能快樂並在學習中實現自我。

整合能力強化 ❹ 參考範文 ▶ *MP3 026*

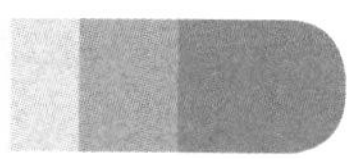

It is true that nowadays kids spend more time on doing lots of activities whether it is the activity assigned by the school or the activity deliberately arranged by some parents. Parents all have good intentions of wanting their kids to start ahead, but it also uncovers something worrisome. In "*How will you Measure Your Life*", the chapter on *sailing your kids on Theseus's ship* reveals worries that might direct us to think about the topic of whether kids should be given more time to do whatever they want.

不論活動是否是由學校所指定的或是活動是由有些父母刻意安排的，現今小孩真的花費更多時間在從事許多活動上。父母有著所有好的意圖，想要他們的孩子在起步上領先，但是這揭露了令人擔憂的部分。在「你如何衡量你的人生」一書中，讓你的孩子航行在賽修斯的船上揭露了擔憂，這能導引我們去思考主題：是否該給予小孩更多時間從事自己想做的事情呢？

It's quite commendable to give children lots of opportunities to explore themselves, but kids can be in the situation as in what the author describes **"parents, often with their heart in the right place, project their own hopes and dreams onto their children"** or **"when these other intentions start creeping in, and parents seem to be charting their**

children around to an endless array of activities in which the kids are not truly engaged…".

相當值得嘉許的是活動能給予小孩更多的機會去自我探索，但是也可能是作者所描述的「父母，通常有著心之所向，將自己本身的希望和夢想投射在自己的小孩上面」或是「當這些其他意圖不知不覺的開始作用時，父母似乎將他們的小孩導向無止盡的活動列表上，但這卻非小孩子真的有意願從事的...」。

Parents' projection or teachers' expectations can harm kids in a certain way, letting kids falsely believe it is something they should do, but years later or after kids have accomplished the degree, they find themselves in an awkward position. Kids specialized in law want to learn business knowledge. In addition, if it is not something kids are passionate about or truly engaged, it can be a total waste of time and money. Arranged activities should be based on kids' interest so that it can maximize the power of learning and benefits for later success.

父母的投射或教師的期望可能在某種程度上傷害著小孩，讓小孩誤以為這些事情是他們應該要做的，但是數年後或是在小孩完成了某個學位後，小孩卻發現自己身處尷尬的處境。精通法律的小孩想要學習商業知識。此外，如果這不是小孩感到熱情的或是實際想從事的，這可能全然浪費時間和金錢。安排活動應該要基於小孩的興趣，如此才能將學習的力量最大化並且有助益於往後的成功。

Back to the topic, I think children should be given more time to do whatever they want because learning should not be arranged. It should be developed. Kids should develop their own interest during leisure time whether it is about finding plants intriguing during trekking with family members or it is about wanting to know more about marine life during the family trips in marine museums. Learning should be spontaneous, and it should not be forced. It should be gradually developed and internally motivated.

回到主題上，我認為應該給予小孩更多時間從事他們所想要做的事，因為學習不該是經由安排的。學習應該是由發展而來的。小孩應該要在閒暇時，發展出自己的興趣，不論是在家庭健行時對植物感到有興趣，或是在海洋博物館的家庭旅遊中，想要更了解關於海洋生活。學習應該是要自動自發的，而非強迫的。學習應該是要逐步發展且是由內部驅策的。

Our brain does need time to rest for optimal functioning. Consume plenty of knowledge rests on that. Only by giving them flexible time to explore what they are truly passionate about and absorb what they have learned during those activities and later focus your sole attention on assisting your kids to achieve their short-term and long-term goals can they have a happier and more fulfilling life.

我們的大腦確實是需要時間休息才能發揮最佳的功用。吸取許多知識還必須要仰賴這點。只有給予孩子們彈性的時間去探索自我，找到真的感到熱忱的事物和吸收他們在那些活動中所學到的，並於稍後將你的重心僅放在協助孩子們達到他們短期和長期目標，這樣他們才能夠有更快樂且實現自我的生活。

UNIT 12 經驗和專業人士：經驗老練的專業人士總是表現得比較年輕的專業人士更好嗎？

Writing Task 2 ▶ *MP3 027*

TOPIC

"Experienced" is a too powerful word used by modern people. Most people are led to believed that experienced professionals, such as doctors and attorneys, perform relatively well than young professionals because they have more experience. What's your opinion?

Write at least 250 words

整合能力強化 ❶ 實際演練

請搭配左頁的題目和並構思和完成大作文的演練。

整合能力強化 ❷ 單句中譯英演練

❶ 他們誤以為較大型的醫院比起小型醫院更好，這樣他們才能受到更良好的治療和照護。

____

____

【參考答案】

They have been misled into believing that bigger hospitals are better the small ones so that they can get better medication and care.

❷ 有些人甚至在網路上做了更小心翼翼的功課，比較著醫生名單，確保他們可以獲得最佳的照護。

____

____

【參考答案】

Some people even do meticulous work by comparing the list of doctors online to ensure they can get the best care possible.

❸ 誤解迴盪在人們心中，而且誤解很難從人們心中剃除。

____

____

【參考答案】

Misconceptions linger in people's mind, and they have become so hard to get rid of.

❹ 儘管許多看似合理的言論蔓延在雙方立場上，相當值得去探討專家所說的，我們才能從中得到關於此現象較合理的結論。

【參考答案】

Although lots of seeming plausible arguments rampant among both sides, it is quite worthwhile to take a look at what experts have to say about this phenomenon so that we can reach a sounder conclusion about it.

❺ 在「刻意練習：來自新科學專業」一書中，它揭露了關於學習上驚人的事實，而且「在幾乎每包含在評論中的六十個研究中，醫生的表現隨著時間而呈現更糟的情況或維持不變」。

【參考答案】

In "*Peak, Secrets from the New Science of Expertise*", it reveals astonishing facts about learning, and "In almost every one of the five dozen studies included in the review, doctors' performance grew worse over time or stayed about the same".

❽「年資較深的醫生所知道的較少而且在提供適當照護上，比起僅有較少年資經驗的醫生表現得更差」。

____

____

【參考答案】

"The older doctors knew less and did worse in terms of providing appropriate care than doctors with far fewer years of experience."

❼「如果持續教育沒有使得醫生有效的精進，那麼隨著年資增長，他們的技能就更落後於現今技術」。

____

____

【參考答案】

"if continuing education does not keep doctors effectively updated, then the order they get, the less current their skill will be".

❽如果事情是這樣的話，那麼具經驗的醫生應該要持續學習新的東西，這樣他們才能夠在表現上超越年輕醫生。

____

____

【參考答案】

If this is the case, then experienced doctors should continue learning new things so that they can still outperform young doctors.

❾ 並不是說具經驗的醫生不是細心的醫生，但是它們傾向認為有些程序是他們一百次了，所以他們沒有像年輕醫生那樣小心翼翼，認為自己不具經驗，所以更該花費更多額外的心力在每個步驟上。

【參考答案】
It is not that experienced doctors are not careful doctors, but they tend to think some procedures as something that they have done them a hundred times, so they are not as careful as young doctors, who are inexperienced so that they put extra attention to every step.

❿ 這些小事情像是投入更多額外的照護或是注意力都可能實際上補足醫療經驗的不足。

【參考答案】
Those little things like putting extra care or attention can actually make up for a lack of experience.

TOPIC

"Experienced" is a too powerful word used by modern people. Most people are led to believed that experienced professionals, such as doctors and attorneys, perform relatively well than young professionals because they have more experience. What's your opinion?

搭配的暢銷書

- Peak, Secrets from the New Science of Expertise 刻意練習：來自新科學專業
- The Millionaire Fastlane 百萬富翁快車道

Step 1 ■ 這題提到經驗還有傳統的刻板印象，以至於大家會認為具專業經驗者比年輕的專業人士表現得更好。

Step 2 ■ 這題蠻難發揮的，而段落首句先以鋪陳的部分講述並反問真的是如此嗎，接著以其中一個行業，醫生的部分為例去討論。

Step 3

■ 提到大家對於大醫院和小醫院的錯誤認知，並指出這些「誤解迴盪在人們心中，而且誤解很難從人們心中剃除。」，最後拉回這個主題。

Step 4

使用暢銷書「刻意練習：來自新科學專業」具體解釋

■「在幾乎每包含在評論中的六十個研究中，醫生的表現隨著時間而呈現更糟的情況或維持不變」。

■「年資較深的醫生所知道的較少而且在提供適當照護上，比起僅有較少年資經驗的醫生表現得更差」。

（這兩句能強化表達，比起僅一般性論述但講不出所以然或很 general 的文法正確文句有效多了）。

Step 5

最後一段更進一步講述「持續的教育是關鍵。」

■「如果持續教育沒有使得醫生有效的精進，那麼隨著年資增長，他們的技能就更落後於現今技術」。

除了講述持續學習，也講到另外幾項重點：

■ 世界是變化的如此快速。

■「具有經驗對一個人來說也可能是巨大的阻撓」，因為他們會有著「我知道自己在做什麼」的觀念存在。

■ 耐心和細心也扮演的關鍵角色。

■ 年輕醫生認為自己不具經驗，所以花費更多額外的心力在每個步驟上。

最後綜合這些因素後作出總結。

It's true that "experienced" means a lot to many people, and it's like a gilded title. People are buying the word "experienced", but do experienced professionals always perform better than younger professionals? I would like to use the profession of doctors as an example to discuss this phenomenon.

對許多人來說，「有經驗」意義重大，這就像是個鍍金的頭銜。人們會因為「經驗老練」而買單，但是具有經驗的專業人士總是表現得比較年輕的專業人士更好嗎？我想要用醫生這個行業為例子來討論這個現象。

Whenever people are getting sick, the first thing that pops into their mind is to go to the hospital, preferably the bigger one. They have been misled into believing that bigger hospitals are better than small ones so that they can get better medication and care. Some people even do meticulous work by comparing the list of doctors online to ensure they can get the best care possible. Misconceptions linger in people's mind, and they have become so hard to get rid of. Sometimes it will lead to a fight between whether bigger hospitals are obviously better or experienced doctors are better than young doctors. These all lead to today's topic of whether experienced professionals are better than young professionals.

每當人們快生病時，突然想到的首要之務是去醫院，且偏好較大型的醫院。他們誤以為較大型的醫院比起小型醫院更好，這樣他們才能受到良好的治療和照護。有些人甚至在網路上做了更小心翼翼的功課，比較著醫生名單，確保他們可以獲得最佳的照護。誤解迴盪在人們心中，而且誤解很難從人們心中剃除。有時候這導致了爭吵，關於較大型的醫院顯然較好或是具經驗的醫生比起年輕醫生來說更好。這些都導向今天的主題，是否具有經驗的專業人士比起較年輕的專業人士來說更好。

Although lots of seeming plausible arguments rampant among both sides, it is quite worthwhile to take a look at what experts have to say about this phenomenon so that we can reach a sounder conclusion. In "*Peak, Secrets from the New Science of Expertise*", it reveals astonishing facts about learning, and **"In almost every one of the five dozen studies included in the review, doctors' performance grew worse over time or stayed about the same"**. "The older doctors knew less and did worse in terms of providing appropriate care than doctors with far fewer years of experience."

儘管許多看似合理的言論蔓延在雙方立場上，相當值得去探討專家所說的，我們才能從中得到關於此現象較合理的結論。在「刻意練習：來自新科學專業」一書中，它揭露了關於學習上驚人的事實，而且「在幾乎每包含在評論中的六十個研究中，醫生的表現隨著時間而呈現更糟的情況或維持不變」。「年資較深的醫生所知道的較少而且在提供適當照護上，比起僅有較少年資經驗的醫生表現的更差」。

This stands in sharp contrast to what people think about experienced doctors. In addition, continual education is the key. **"if continuing education does not keep doctors effectively updated, then the order they get, the less current their skill will be"**. This applies to every profession because **"the world is in constant flux, and it evolves your education must move with it or you will drift to mediocrity."** New skills will become obsolete in such a short time. If this is the case, then experienced doctors should continue learning new things so that they can still outperform young doctors.

這與人們對於具經驗的醫生所了解的全然不同。此外，持續的教育是關鍵。「如果持續教育沒有使得醫生有效的精進，那麼隨著年資增長，他們的技能就更落後於現今技術」。這能應用於每個職業中，因為「這個世界不斷地演進，而你的教育必須要跟著成長，否則你就會落入平庸之中。」新技能可能在短時間內就過時了。如果事情是這樣的話，那麼具經驗的醫生應該要持續學習新的東西，這樣他們才能夠在表現上超越年輕醫生。

Also, they should stay humble. Experienced can be a great hindrance for a person since they have the mindset of "I know what I am doing". Patience and carefulness are also the key. It is not that experienced doctors are not careful doctors, but they tend to think of some procedures as something that they have performed a hundred times, so they are not as careful as young doctors, who are inexperienced so that they put extra attention to every step. Keep in mind that in the courtroom a mistake in thousands of operations is still considered a mistake, and an error can result in regrettable harm. Those little things like putting extra care or attention can actually make up for a lack of experience. To sum up, with all reasons mentioned above, I do not agree that experienced professionals are better than young professionals.

而且，他們應該要保持謙虛。具有經驗對一個人來說也可能是巨大的阻撓，因為他們抱持著「我知道自己在做什麼」的心態。耐心和細心也扮演的關鍵角色。並不是說具經驗的醫生不是細心的醫生，但是它們傾向認為有些程序他們執行過一百次了，所以他們沒有像年輕醫生那樣小心翼翼，認為自己不具經驗，所以更該花費更多額外的心力在每個步驟上。要記住的是在法庭上，一千次手術中有一次失誤仍被視為是疏失，而且一個錯誤可能導致令人感到遺憾的傷害。這些小事情像是投入更多額外的照護或是注意力都可能實際上補足醫療經驗的不足。總之，基於上述這些所有理由，我不同意具經驗的專業人士表現得比年輕的專業人士更好。

雅思寫作模擬試題 引用頁面

書籍／影集	引述句
An Economist Walks into a Brothel	*"de-risking increases the odds of getting what you want, but you must give up the probability of getting more."*
First Jobs	*"These cucumbers were in good shape but they could not be shipped because they had been in the cooler for long."*
How Will You Measure Your Life	*"The only way to be truly satisfied is to do what you believe is great work. And the only way to do great work is to love what you do."*
The Promise of the Pencil	● *"There actually will be times in life when you should choose money over experience"* ● *"but make that choice when the margin is much bigger, when the margin is millions of dollars, not thousand."*
Rich Dad Poor Dad	● *"Often in the real world, it's not the smart who get ahead, but the bold."* ● *"Winners are not afraid of losing. But losers are."*
The Defining Decade	*"For those who have a growth mindset, failures may sting but they are also viewed as opportunities for improvement and change."*
Mistakes I Made at Work	● *"When you have a "growth mindset", you understand that mistakes and setbacks are an inevitable part of learning."* ● *"The idea of "work-life balance" is not necessarily helpful. If you are immersed in your work and raising a family, you might feel a lot of good things...."*
The Job	*"the more you talk about work-life balance, the more you create the problem that you want to solve."*

書籍／影集	引述句
Desperate Housewives	● *"I have four kids under the age of six. I absolutely have anger management issue"* ● *"if I threw a little slower, then it would be playing bowling."*
First Jobs	*"had the rest of my life to work, and I should just study and enjoy life now."*
Getting There	*"Many students are so focused on getting the right grades so that they can get into the right school that it barely gives them the chance to do something zany."*
How You Measure Your Life	*"parents, often with their heart in the right place, project their own hopes and dreams onto their children"* *"when these other intentions start creeping in, and parents seem to be charting their children around to an endless...".*
Peak, Secrets from the New Science of Expertise	*"In almost every one of the five dozen studies included in the review, doctors' performance grew worse over time or stayed about the same".* *"The older doctors knew less and did worse in terms of providing appropriate care than doctors with far fewer years of experience."* *"if continuing education does not keep doctors effectively updated, then the order they get, the less current their skill will be".*
The Millionaire Fastlane	*"the world is in constant flux, and it evolves your education must move with it or you will drift to mediocrity."*

國家圖書館出版品預行編目(CIP)資料

雅思寫作聖經：模擬試題/韋爾著. -- 初版.--
新北市 : 倍斯特出版事業有限公司, 2022.11
面； 公分. --（考用英語系列 ; 041）
ISBN 978-626-96563-1-8 (平裝)
1.CST: 國際英語語文測試系統 2.CST: 作文

805.189 111017226

考用英語系列 041

雅思寫作聖經-模擬試題（英式發音附QR code音檔）

初　刷　2022年11月
定　價　新台幣530元

作　者　韋爾
出　版　倍斯特出版事業有限公司
發行人　周瑞德
電　話　886-2-8245-6905
傳　真　886-2-2245-6398
地　址　23558 新北市中和區立業路83巷7號4樓
E-mail　best.books.service@gmail.com
官　網　www.bestbookstw.com
總編輯　齊心瑀
封面構成　高鍾琪
內頁構成　菩薩蠻數位文化有限公司
印　製　大亞彩色印刷製版股份有限公司

港澳地區總經銷　泛華發行代理有限公司
地　址　香港新界將軍澳工業邨駿昌街7號2樓
電　話　852-2798-2323
傳　真　852-3181-3973